Fantastically Horny

A Far Horizons Press Anthology

Far Horizons Press
FAR HORIZONS is a FREE eMagazine, brought about from a simple idea to let unpublished, thinly published and self-published writers and artists showcase their work to the World.
The first issue was released on the 17th of April, 2014.
Far Horizons Press grew out of the magazine with a desire to bring the very best stories into print. Far Horizons Press titles are designed to provide a much needed income stream so we can continue to offer the magazine free of charge and continue to develop our writers and artists.

Fantastically Horny

Edited by

Dirk Spearman and Mistress Lapis

Far Horizons Press

Fantastically Horny
Edited by Dirk Spearman and Mistress Lapis
Published by Stacey Welsh
Cover art Cover photos purchased from depositphotos.com
designed by SJR cover design
First Edition Published
by Far Horizons Press
25 Jul 2015
This edition TBC

Visit our website

CONTENTS

Fantastically Horny

Introduction

By Stacey Welsh

Sex... The final, orgasmic frontier.

Ever since the first person decided to put sex on paper, erotica works have been tantalizing and terrifying people all over the world. Erotica has been both banned and enjoyed all over the world. From early erotic poetry of the Greeks and Romans to literary masterpieces like *The Decameron* (1353) by the Italian Giovanni Boccaccio, to the works of Edmund Curll (1675–1747), and works like *The Romance of Lust* (1873), *The Autobiography of a Flea* (1887), *The Sins of the Cities of the Plain* (1881), *Suburban Souls* (1901), *The Confessions of Nemesis Hunt* (issued in three volumes 1902, 1903, 1906) probably by George Reginald Bacchus, erotica has had a very fruitful history.

Contributing to this incredible array of works, is this collection of short stories titled *Fantastically Horny.*

These are the stories of sexual adventures, fantastical cultural lives and new beginnings in the journey to erotic awareness, sorted into two groups according to their genre – *Horny Fantasy* and *Horny Sci-fi.*

Read on as we enter into a parallel universe, in the realm of fantasy, where we discover that Centaurs are really hung like a horse in *The Olive Harvest.* Up the road in Camelot, the maidens are playing with some very hot magic in *Camelot Girls Gone Wild,* and a devious Seductress meets her match in *King and Queen.* We take a trip to visit some clans in *The Fourth Husband,* we take a ride with dragons in *Dragon's Mate,* join a search for a precious item in *Passion Skull,* and follow a man given as tribute to a strange creature in *Cleopticus and Haerne.*

We travel through time in the comic that separates the two story groups, *Love in Zero Gravity.*

Then we take a right turn to intergalactic romance and erotic situations as we blast through the wormhole in our long, sleek and hard as steel spaceship, thrusters at full towards such erotic tales as *My First Alien*, where we discover that alien abductions can be fun, while an alien visitor offers more than first contact in *Subject 93-A*. We wonder what is stronger, love or attraction in *Mind over Matter*, we see what it takes to start a business in *The Permit*, we go to where fighting and flirting meet in *Hot Summer*, and we see where the last sip of water ends up in *Drip*.

Head on down to the galactic academy where three cadets discover the delicious mysteries of alien lovemaking in *The Way You Make Me feel*, before we undock and fly towards Jupiter in *:ove at Solar System's End*, and we see what happened with all the wine in *Clurichaun*.

What sensual escapades lie beyond these Far Horizons?

Strap on, lie back aboard your spaceship or your dragon and find out!

Horny Fantasy

The Fourth Husband

By Rose Hill

Ilker's excitement over killing his first river-dog lasted until they returned home and he found one of the matriarch's young husbands waiting for him. With his beard just long enough to braid, the boy was younger than Ilker, barely old enough to marry. The youth sneered at their unkempt appearance.

"Matriarch Dilek requires your presence," the boy sniffed. "Do be sure to wash yourself first."

Ilker grinned and looped an arm around the boy, pulling him close. The messenger winced as Ilker rubbed his dirty, sweaty beard in the boy's hair. His fathers and uncles laughed as the boy squirmed away. "Don't worry, city-boy. We know how to be civilized."

Ilker let him go, and the boy-toy ran off. In high spirits, Ilker headed off to the bathing room with the other men. Everyone had survived this expedition, returning safely home with rare pelts and vials of flesh-dissolving spider venom to sell.

But the messenger made Ilker nervous. Though she was his grandmother, he had never needed to deal with the matriarch directly. Any orders, punishments, or commendations came from his mother, Ilknur Magara, or more likely his fathers and uncles. What had he done to attract the matriarch's attention?

He dressed in his best clothes and braided his beard in the clan pattern before heading up to see his grandmother. Spelled crystals set in reflective niches shed a steady light through tunnel-like staircases. At the top of the highest staircase, he knocked on the ceiling, the door to the matriarch's study.

"Come in!"

Ilker opened the door and climbed into the matriarch's room. His grandmother sat at the desk writing on a slate. Her curly hair was trying to escape its salt-and-pepper braid and her skin had the delicate, pale look of a woman who never saw the sun. The Magara clan made its living from the caves. Her favourite husband, Erol Irmak, sat beside her and watched as Ilker carefully made his bow. Originally from a travelling clan, Erol had the broad features and curly dark hair that could match a dwarven man in any city.

"Matriarch Dilek," Ilker said. "You wished to see me?"

"Ilknur Magara-oglu Ilker Magara." The casual statement of his full name only added to his confusion. He couldn't read her emotions. He still had no idea why she wanted to see him. She finally looked up from her writing to pierce him with her dark-eyed gaze. "You survived. Good. Step forward."

Ilker approached the edge of her desk. What was this for? He did not seem to be in trouble. If this was about the river-dog, that was a fairly minor feat. Certainly nothing worth of being called before the matriarch.

She passed him a carved tablet of red and black spotted granite. "Read this." She waited until he was halfway through before adding, "And congratulations."

His hands clenched on the stone. He was getting married? Ilker pressed his lips together to prevent anything inappropriate from slipping out as he read through the rest of the slab. He had thought the plan to rebuild the clan's standing involved sending the men out to raid the Tainted Lands. Considering the high losses involved in such an endeavour, the daughters of the Magara clan married as many husbands as they could afford and the sons stayed in the family. Ilker was his mother's oldest child. He had expected to spend his life raiding the Tainted Lands with the men of his clan. He would have been happy that way.

Why marry him off now? And the choice of clan was... interesting. The Tunc clan was infamous for their distaste of anything human. Why would they want to associate with a disgraced clan that regularly ventured into human lands? And why offer such a favourable trade agreement?

Aware of the matriarch and her favoured husband's gaze on him, Ilker lifted his eyes and asked the only acceptable question. "When do I leave?"

***

Ilker thanked the men of the Irmak clan who had travelled with him from Haynurdamla to Berrakirmdor. The city glittered with mottled black and white granite, a twisting array of steps, avenues and homes carved into the living rock of the mountain. The symbol of the powerful – and extremely wealthy – Elmas clan appeared on public works everywhere he looked: a perfect hexagonal prism laid over a mountain. The Tunc clan saw themselves as rivals of Elmas, but no other clan approached the Elmas level of wealth. Why had his matriarch created an alliance with such an ambitious family?

"Ilknur Magara-oglu Ilker Magara!"

Ilker started at the sound of his name and looked to see a stout dwarf armed like a Demir scowling at him. An older man, his black hair just starting to gray, he bore the muscles of one who exercised but never put practice to use. Ilker stood before him and waited for the older man to introduce himself. The man looked him up and down, clicking his tongue.

"Yet another pretty-boy," he said with a sigh. "Figures." Ilker crossed his arms and refused to rise to the bait. The man waited a moment, then grunted and introduced himself. "I'm Dilara Tunc-koca Kadir Demir, Dilara's first husband. So you'll have to listen to me." Kadir paused to glare at him.

"Of course," Ilker said mildly. "That is typically how it works." And Demir clan before marriage; he'd called it correctly. At Kadir's increasing glare, Ilker tried to redirect the conversation. "How many husbands does she have?"

Kadir grunted again and started walking. Ilker quickly adjusted his pack and followed. "You're the fourth. She isn't too excited to have yet another mouth to feed, so don't be surprised if she refuses you outright."

"I can carry my own weight," Ilker protested, stung. He brushed his fingers against the scales of his river-dog skin cloak and reminded himself not to snap at his senior husband.

"That's for Dilara to decide." Kadir said little else as they walked to the Tunc clan house. Ilker studied the city as they walked, to distract himself from the potential loss of a trade agreement if Dilara rejected him. The Tunc clan symbol, an intricate interlocking knot, featured here and there, but it was nowhere near as prevalent as the Elmas symbol. No doubt it grated on the Tunc clan to walk by their rival's paid works day after day.

The home of the Tunc clan rose, towering above them, carved knot work curling around the door. Kadir allowed Ilker not one moment to admire it before bustling him inside to the bathing room. Ilker cleaned off the road dust and made himself presentable. But when he went to pick up his pack again Kadir stopped him.

"Leave that here. The servants will bring it to the men's room. Just grab your tablet out of it. The matriarch is waiting for you."

Ilker grabbed his marriage tablet and followed Kadir. Like his clan house back home, the matriarch's office was the highest room in the house. Up and up they went, until finally they reached her room. The matriarch sat alone at her desk while two guards from the Demir clan stood at attention on either side of the door. Ilker dropped his eyes to keep from staring. Female guards were expensive.

"You must be Ilker Magara, once of Ilknur Magara." Her

strong, clear voice filled the room. She could not have been much older than his own grandmother, but he knew from his history lessons she had been the matriarch of her clan much longer.

"Yes, matriarch." He approached her desk with eyes bowed and offered her the tablet.

Matriarch Asli Tunc read through the tablet and nodded briskly. She set the stone down and passed him bronze beard twists, a stamped symbol of the Tunc clan hanging from the bottom. "Welcome to the family, Dilara Tunc-koca Ilker Magara."

His wife was supposed to be the one to welcome him to the family, but he dared not argue. "Thank you, matriarch." He twisted the mark of his marital status into his beard.

"Now," she said, leaning back and steepling her fingers. "I suppose you're wondering which of these lovely two women is Dilara."

Ilker paused and blinked up at her. He looked back, but the only other women in the room were the guards. "I would not ask such a rude question. Though I find it hard to believe that any women of the estimable Tunc clan would be allowed to look like a Demir."

Matriarch Asli laughed. "It's good to see there's still some education going on in that old ruin. You'll do just fine here. Kadir, take him to meet your brother-husbands. And try not to scare him too much."

Kadir bowed respectfully, but a thread of anger heated his, "Yes, matriarch." Ilker risked flashing a smile at his new matriarch before following his senior husband out. Once they were well out of hearing range, Kadir stopped and turned to Ilker. "Don't think you'll get ahead just because the matriarch likes you. It's Dilara you have to impress."

Ilker met his eyes and refused to be intimidated. "I know

who my wife is," he said, utterly ignoring the irony of that statement. "Speaking of, when am I going to meet her? She has to accept me for me to officially be part of the clan, right?"

Kadir huffed and started walking again. "Yes. The matriarch likes to ignore that fact, but you're on probation until Dilara accepts you. Screw it up and whatever alliance your worthless clan argued for crumbles like sand."

Ilker followed him, more concerned with Kadir's attitude than his threat. While there were certainly those who viewed their brother-husbands as rivals, most tried to cooperate for the benefit of their shared wife. While Ilker had never expected to be married off, since hearing the news he hoped for husbands with whom he could practice. That looked increasingly unlikely.

On the same floor as the bathing room, Kadir opened a door without knocking. Two men sat on either side of a game-rug, playing pieces scattered over its surface. One was short, even for a dwarf, with the smooth hair that could only be from Sedadeniz, on the coast. The other was well built, with sun-kissed skin and the kinky hair Ilker expected in a dwarf. Both looked up as Kadir shoved Ilker inside.

"Dilara's been given a new one," Kadir said, ignoring the glare Ilker shot him. "Meet Ilker Magara, your newest brother-husband. This is Halim Shule and Altan Sedir, formerly the most junior husband."

The Shule clan harvested pearls and abalone in Sedadeniz, so he'd called that one right. Sedir was not a clan name Ilker recognized, though judging from the sun-kissed skin he guessed Altan was from one of the clans that farmed the heavily guarded mountain valleys. Altan leaned back from the game. "Kadir, don't tell me you're mistreating our husbands again. Ilker, come here."

"I wouldn't say mistreated," Ilker hedged as he retrieved his pack from where he spotted it along the wall.

"I do not mistreat," Kadir said stiffly, at the same time.

"Oh, don't mind Kadir," Altan told Ilker as he sat to observe the game board. "He's just bitter because Dilara likes him least."

All three winced at the loud reverberation of the door slamming against stone.

"Altan, that was rude," Halim chided.

"Kadir is rude," Altan said with a roll of his eyes. "It's only fair if we're rude back sometimes. So. Magara." He glanced at Ilker. "Where is that from?"

"Haynurdamla," Halim answered, moving a piece.

"Know-it-all," Altan muttered, moving a stone in retaliation.

"He's right, though," Ilker said as Halim studied the board. "Clan Magara has always been in Haynurdamla."

"Why does that sound familiar?" Altan wondered.

"Because you were theoretically taught history at some point," Halim said dryly. He moved another piece.

Altan snapped his fingers. "That's it! You used to trade with humans way back when. You're an odd choice to marry in to the Tunc clan." He moved a piece after barely glancing at the board.

"We haven't traded with humans in centuries," Ilker said. "Not since they destroyed the eastern city with their wars. Though I won't deny it's strange."

"Huh. Why do you think the Tunc would accept him, Halim?"

"Because they haven't traded with humans in centuries. And their matriarch is extremely clever." Halim pointed at

Ilker's side without lifting his eyes from the game board. "Do you recognize this material?"

"No." Altan leaned over to examine Ilker's cloak, trailing his fingers down Ilker's arm. Ilker watched him with amusement. Only among family was such intimacy allowed. Husbands counted, even if they were strangers. Altan glanced up and met his eyes with a wicked smile. Ilker was sure Altan knew what he was thinking. "So, what is it?"

Ilker had to clear his throat before he could speak. "River-dog. From the caves of the Tainted Lands. I killed this one myself."

Altan examined the cloak again with a frown. "Dogs don't have scales."

"River-dogs aren't actually dogs," Ilker said. "They're more like canine snakes. Dog-like in form, but with scales, claws and venom."

"Venom?"

Ilker nodded. "They're not as bad as cave spiders, though. The venom from those things will dissolve flesh in a matter of minutes."

"And that's why Ilker is now a Tunc," Halim said. "Exclusive trade rights to extremely rare items." He looked up and caught Altan's eyes. "Victory in four moves. Would you like me to list them?"

Altan waved his hand and let Halim start picking up the pieces. "Bah. You always beat me anyways." He nudged Ilker with his elbow. "Come on. I'll show you where you can put your things." Opening a door in the back, he pulled up the edge of a lantern. Half a dozen low beds lined the walls. Altan pointed out which were claimed as he closed the door behind him.

"Seriously though," Altan said as Ilker picked a bed, "don't mind Kadir. He's bitter that being first doesn't make him the favourite. He treats the whole thing like a competition, as if we're not all in the same clan together. And Dilara is fair; she'll give you your chance."

"When will I get to meet her? No one's said yet."

Altan's eyes widened. "You didn't meet her before they wrote the contract? That's rude of the matriarchs." He sighed. "Then again, that's what Kadir and Halim said about their marriages to her as well. I had hoped the matriarchs were getting better about that." He shook his head. "Dilara rotates through us so that it's fair to everyone. Tonight is Halim's night with her. Mine's after that. I imagine you'll probably be tacked on after me."

Ilker nodded. Two days. He had two days to figure out how to impress his new wife. He had no idea what he was supposed to do.

"Nervous?" Altan asked. His grin was back.

"Yes," Ilker answered honestly. He could not decide whether that was too much time, or not enough. She already had three husbands. What could he learn in two days that would impress her?

"Don't be," Altan said, shaking his head. "Dilara's not that scary. Make her laugh, get her to relax a bit, you'll be fine. She already has two serious husbands. She doesn't need a third."

"Is that what makes you the favourite?" Ilker asked impudently. He opened the trunk at the foot of his new bed and knelt to unpack his things.

Altan laughed. "Of course. Wouldn't I be your favourite too?"

Ilker grinned. "I don't know, I should really give the others a chance. Get to know them a bit."

"Aw, but they won't let you practice with them like I will."

Ilker sat up straight. "Will you?"

Altan laughed. "Yes, I will." He crossed the room and sat on the bed Ilker chose. "And I shouldn't laugh – I know how Kadir comes off." He leaned over and pressed a kiss to Ilker's lips. "I'm sorry." Altan kissed him again and Ilker leaned in to it, trying to deepen the kiss. Altan pulled back again. "And Halim will probably practice with you too, but he's shy so you'll have to seduce him first, and I don't think you'll have time for—"

Shrugging off his cloak, Ilker interrupted him with a kiss. Altan put his hand around the back of Ilker's neck and opened his lips, letting their tongues dance together. Ilker rose to his knees and turned to face him. This was the sort of practice he'd been hoping for with his husbands. Altan's hand slid down his neck to his back. Ilker took the subtle pressure as encouragement and crawled over Altan, pushing him back against the bed. Altan pulled Ilker's tunic off.

The movement gave them a moment to breathe. Altan trailed a finger down a line of puckered skin. "What are the scars from?"

"Fighting in the caves of the Tainted Lands." Ilker propped himself up on one arm, body hovering just above his. He slid his other hand up Altan's tunic as he kissed him again.

"I thought you said that stuff was poisonous," he gasped as his hands slid down to Ilker's pants.

"Venomous. But not everything." Ilker pulled Altan's tunic off.

"But—"

"Do you ever stop talking?" Ilker asked, trying not to laugh.

Altan grinned. "No."

Kissing him, Ilker decided Altan would, in fact, be

excellent practice. If he could manage to distract a man this talkative, he should be able to distract anyone. But with Altan's hands on his hips and his pants already halfway off, it was Ilker who was getting distracted.

Ilker shimmied back out of reach, pulling Altan's pants down with him. He misremembered where the edge of the bed was and teetered precariously. Altan sat up in alarm. "Careful."

Ilker kissed him to cut off any further words. Back down on to the bed they went, and Ilker wrapped his hand around Altan's now exposed cock. Altan shivered underneath him, already rock hard, warm and smooth in his hand.

"That's not exactly practice," Altan breathed.

"Are you complaining?" Ilker knelt down and licked the firm head of his penis.

"Goddess, no. But the point was for you to learn something." Despite his words, Altan's hand on the back of his neck encouraged him to continue. Ilker made a noncommittal sound and licked the length of his cock, circling slowly all the way around. Altan's hand tightened in Ilker's hair. Ilker licked the tip of his shaft but found himself suddenly shy.

"What sort of practice were you thinking of?"

Altan put a hand on his cheek and drew him up for a chaste kiss. "Strip."

While Ilker shivered out of his pants, Altan crossed over to another bed and returned with a bottle.

"The kind of practice," Altan said, interspersing his words with kisses, "that you'll want," he opened the bottle, "in a couple of days with Dilara." Altan's hand wrapped around Ilker's cock, coating him with oil. Ilker shivered with sudden understanding. He put his hands on Altan's hips and pushed him back against the bed. Altan spread his legs on either side of Ilker and pulled him down for a kiss.

Ilker repositioned himself and pressed inside him before any second thoughts could assail him. It was surprisingly easy. "Like this?"

Altan raised his hips to meet him. "Yes." His hands were tight on Ilker's arms. "Yes. Just like that."

It was intoxicating to have a lover stretched out beneath him as Ilker moved inside him. He ran his fingers through curls of dark hair on Altan's chest, following the trail down to where his cock pressed against Ilker's stomach. Wrapping his hand around Altan's cock, Ilker stroked him in time to his thrusts. Altan moved his hand to Ilker's back to help control the timing. The feel of Altan tight around him was too much for Ilker to last. As he shuddered into his husband, Altan wrapped his hand over Ilker's on his cock. Ilker pulled himself together long enough to get Altan off. He pulled out as Altan came, squirting all over their hands.

Ilker flopped down on the bed, breathing hard.

"Now that," Altan said with a satisfied smile, "is practice."

***

Ilker spent the next day with Halim, inventorying the trade goods he brought as part of the marriage agreement. Halim asked intelligent questions about their uses and took detailed notes. But every time Ilker tried to flirt or ask questions about him, Halim turned shy. If he was going to seduce this husband of his, Ilker would have to get him to relax a bit first. To put him at ease, Ilker told him stories about the Tainted caves: water that flowed the wrong way; stones that emitted light, darkness, heat, and cold; unnaturally large spiders; caverns full of magic-absorbing crystals; vicious steel-bears; wandering forests of mushrooms; and the broken ruins of human and dwarven settlements.

Halim seemed much more comfortable that evening in the men's room, so Ilker assumed his stories had helped. After playing a few games on the game-rug, Ilker quickly discovered why Altan always lost. Ilker managed to win two games, though he could not say whether that was due to skill, luck or Halim throwing the game. That man was good.

It was an enjoyable evening, despite the constant presence of Kadir's glare and the lack of Altan's laughter.

In the morning, Ilker and Halim finished the inventory. Setting aside for the moment his plans of seducing his shy husband, Ilker questioned Halim about their wife. Halim seemed as averse to discuss Dilara as he had been to discuss himself the day before, but here Ilker did not hesitate to press for details. He would need them later.

The day seemed to alternatively crawl and fly by. His nervousness steadily increased. He had no idea how he was supposed to win her favour. If Dilara didn't accept him, his clan's trade agreement would fall through. Pleasing her was Magara's best chance at regaining their former glory.

Altan and Halim both tried to reassure him, but before he left for her, Kadir stopped him and whispered, "Be nervous." Ilker went to meet his wife muttering uncomplimentary things about his senior husband.

Dilara sat in her sitting room, reading wax tablets in a bright red woollen dressing gown. Her black hair, shining red in the light of the spelled crystals on the walls, was silky and straight like a dwarf from Sedadeniz, though Ilker doubted she had ever been outside of Berrakirmdor. She was broad and well-curved, like the Goddess in her most beautiful depictions. How the humans and elves found anything attractive in their stick-like women Ilker would never understand.

"Ilknur Magara-oglu Ilker Magara." Her voice was sweet and smooth as berry-wine, but she spoke his old name, marking him as his mother's son rather than her wife.

Correcting her might get him in trouble, but he wanted to reinforce that he belonged to her now. "Dilara Tunc-koca Ilker Magara," he said softly.

Her lips twitched, eyes flicking from his face to his Tunc beard twist and back. "Indeed."

Well, he didn't seem to be in trouble yet. He moved behind her chair. She watched him warily, but voiced no objections. Brushing her hair forward, he rubbed her shoulders. She closed her eyes and relaxed against the chair. This wasn't so bad.

"Your notes in the inventory should be useful," she said after a few minutes.

"Thank you. May I ask what they'll be useful for?"

"Where we'll market the Magara products. It's my trade agreement to manage. That's why you're mine." She opened her eyes and looked up at him.

That possessiveness boded well for her willingness to keep him. "What are you going to do with me now?"

She smiled and he could see why Altan was her favourite. They had the same mischievous look. "Maybe I want to see what else you'll be useful for."

He smiled and withdrew his hands. Following her into the bedroom, she closed the sides of the spelled crystal and closed the door, shrouding the room in darkness. Ilker paused, uncertain and blinded.

"This way." Unseen hands pulled and prodded him across the room. She pinched and tugged at his clothes, so that he was in a state of disarray by the time his legs hit the bed. Ilker caught the next hands that tried to touch him. He kissed the backs of the hands and continued up the arms. Somewhere in the darkness Dilara had dropped her dressing gown. He suddenly felt distinctly over-dressed. He let go and quickly stripped off his tunic.

She pushed him on to the bed and straddled him. "You're still too dressed."

"I'm noticing that." When had it become hard to breathe? He had to focus if he wanted to impress her. Or at least not embarrass himself. Right now he would settle for that. He tried to reach down to his pants, but found her smooth skin instead. He followed the skin upwards before he realized what he was doing and yanked his hands away.

Dilara chuckled. "You are allowed to touch me, husband." Moving away in the darkness, she tugged at his pants. He quickly pulled them off and tossed them to the side. Reaching for where he thought she was, he found her silky hair and followed it to cup her face. Her cheek was smooth beneath his rough hands, so he kept his touch light as he followed her chin to the corner of her mouth. He licked his lips, leaned in, and gently pressed his lips to hers. She returned the kiss with ardour, sliding her hand up the curls of his chest hair to rest on his shoulder.

Then she shoved him.

He fell back on to a surprisingly nice bed, softer than anything they had in the men's quarters. But he had no time to consider that as she straddled him. He wrapped his hands around her waist, delighting in the feel of her skin against his hands. Breasts, sides, back, hips, he explored wherever he could reach. Her hair framed her face as she leaned over to kiss him.

He squirmed underneath her, wanting to be inside her. She sat up a bit, pulling out of his hands, then came back down on top of him. Ilker gasped as he slid inside her. So soft and wet. She moved against him and his breath caught, thrusting inside her. Leaning over, she braced herself on his chest, twining her fingers in his chest hair. With his hands on her hips, she ground against him as he thrust up to meet her. Faster and faster as her fingers tightened on him. He stroked her thighs where they wrapped around him, trying to last long enough for her pleasure. When she arched and cried out, he could not last any more.

She climbed off of him and collapsed on the bed, breathing hard. Ilker tugged a blanket out and tossed it over them.

"I think you'll be useful," she said when she caught her breath again. "Welcome to the family."

Ilker smiled. Between his wife and his husbands, he was going to enjoy married life.

Dragon's Mate

By Beatrice Wolfe

The dragon lowered its huge head and inhaled slowly through wide, quivering nostrils.

"Hmm," he ruminated. "What have we here? I ask for the small matter of one maiden each month, to be delivered to me, to keep me from wreaking fiery havoc on the town. But you, if my senses don't deceive me, are not quite a maiden."

"I'm afraid you are right," spoke the woman doing her best to stand tall in the face of the large, brown dragon. "Quite a long way from being a maiden, if truth be told. I'm afraid you've been short-changed. I think you'd be well within your rights to fly straight to the village and start burning down every building. I wouldn't blame you at all. In fact, if you could just untie me and let me put some clothes back on I could point you in the right direction."

"I know the way," said the dragon.

The dragon blinked slowly and then exhaled out a warm, but not flaming, breath. He stared at the woman before him. She was red haired, almond eyed and full breasted. She was a woman, not a girl, and, the dragon knew, met all the criteria for what humans perceived as beautiful. She was held captive by dint of having her arms tied behind her to the same stake where some scores of others had been tied before.

"To be honest, the maiden thing was just for the sake of tradition," said the dragon. "It really doesn't make any difference to me. You're not the first. Maidens seem to have become somewhat scarce in the town of late."

"Do you think the possibility of being sacrificed to a fire-breathing dragon might be something of a disincentive for a girl to remain virgo intacto? The young lads of the town raise a glass to you on a weekly basis. Your presence in the valley has saved them having to take dancing lessons or spending large amounts of money on alcohol."

A throaty noise that might have been a laugh emitted from the back of the dragon's throat. A forked tongue slipped in and out through jagged teeth.

"You amuse me," said the dragon. "I might keep you alive a while yet."

"Well, I'm sure I can be amusing for a very long time. I could be even more amusing if my arms and legs were free. I could tell you a story I heard once. There was this hero who set out to fight a dragon. They fought until the hero found a gap in the scales through which he could plunge a sword. Must have been a pretty stupid hero. Anyone can see you don't have any scales where your bollocks are. Although I do notice that your cock is somewhat relaxed at the moment. Clearly, despite my unclothed state, I don't appeal to you. Why not just let me go?"

The dragon raised its front limb. He unsheathed a claw which he used to trace a line down the cheek of the woman. Even with the flat back of the claw, a pinprick of blood started to run down her face.

"We'll see," said the dragon, at which point he spread his vast wings and flew up and over the ridge.

The woman lent back against the stake which held her. Despite her exposed situation, a smile lit up her face. She didn't try and pull free of the ropes that held her but waited with a confidence that something would happen.

The day was starting to turn to sunset when she finally heard the sound she had been waiting for. A flurry of stones rolled down the side of the slope away to her side. These were followed by the arms, legs and body of a human male.

"I came as fast as I could."

"I felt sure you would," replied the woman. She smiled in

greeting at the young man who ran towards her. His brown hair flew backwards with the speed of his approach. As soon as he reached her he kissed her full on the lips.

"That's all very well, but could you untie me first?"

The young man fumbled at the knots until he eventually loosed enough of them that the woman was able to get free. As soon as she stepped away from the wooden stake, he threw his arms around her. This time she returned the kiss.

"Don't you want to get away from here?" she asked. "Dragons are not known for looking kindly on men who take what they believe to be theirs."

"I don't care."

The woman pulled at the fastenings of his tunic. "Well, if you're sure." She tugged the tunic up over the man's head and started kissing his chest. As he ran his hands down her back, she pushed him away with more strength than he expected. He landed hard on the ground, looking up with a puzzled expression. She stepped forward so that she was standing over him, her feet planted either side of his hips. The woman smiled as she saw him brazenly admire her body. She knelt down, leaning forward so that her breasts hung above his face. He took the prompt and kissed each of her nipples in turn. When he tried to reach a hand up to pull her closer, she slapped it aside. The woman arched her back, in the process accentuating her figure to full advantage. She slid her knees backwards until they were alongside his. As she locked eyes with the man, she slowly licked her lips. Her fingers danced a pattern in the air between them before she started to use them to untie the knot that held his breeches tight at the waist.

Soon, the young man was as naked as the woman and lying on the grassy bank while she straddled his stomach, back turned toward him, and her fingers wrapped around his phallus. He did not ejaculate all too quickly, as most men she had known. Instead the erect member started to grow even bigger. She turned her head and looked teasingly over her shoulder at the face that was changing form before her eyes.

"I wondered how long you'd manage to hold out," said the woman.

"You knew?" said the no longer human voice, of the no longer young man. "All the time?"

"All the time," replied the woman. "Right back to the hayloft."

The woman kept her balance, sitting on the expanding belly of the young man as he completed his metamorphosis back into the form of the brown dragon.

"How?" asked the dragon.

The woman put her arms around the still erect member to steady herself as she stood up and turned around. She ran her hands through her red hair and smiled down at the reptilian face.

"How else," she said as she in turn started to grow and change.

The red-scaled female dragon that lay atop the younger brown grew until her size was larger by a third again. Her clawed limbs pinned his to the ground.

"But that is not the question you really want to ask right now," she said as she put her face next to his. "What you should really be asking is why you've never met any other dragons before me. How could you be the last of the dragons when you are so powerful? What is the meaning of your life?"

She started to mate with him, undulating rhythmically up and down, in full control of her situation. His reaction was both inevitable and involuntary.

"Let me tell you," said the red dragon. "The meaning of

your life is no more than this."

As they continued to mate the red dragon raised her head and breathed down on him. The flames from her mouth consumed his flesh. As his body reached a final shudder, his head was already a pile of ashes.

Passion Skull

By W.H. Hamilton

In the lowest part of the castle, in the coldest corner of the under-hall, the skull resided. I had spent nearly six months as a slave in the dank castle on the frozen Borzick Islands searching for the skull. The hours felt like weeks, and the weeks like years as I was demeaned, harassed, and worked to the bone – all so Lord Farshaw could fulfil his disturbed fantasies of having a female gnome as a slave.

But I hadn't given into his deepest of fantasies. I couldn't stand the thought of him running his wrinkled, calloused hands over my naked body, stroking my silken auburn hair. I shuddered at the thought of his shrivelled, human member inside me.

No, he had tried many times. I had always refused.

Finally, he had insisted. He thought he could force me, thought he could overpower me simply because of my small stature. When he dropped his pants, exposing himself to me, I used all my strength to crush his pitiful manhood between my fingers – no better than a couple raisins and a small rotted banana.

***

I stood at the bottom of the stone staircase and peered into the dimly illuminated under-hall. This was my final chance to find the skull.

After this, if Lord Farshaw caught me, I'd be exiled from the Borzick Islands – or worse, he would have me killed. I tried not to let myself consider worse scenarios.

I held up the lantern (almost half my size and cumbersome to carry) as I made my way across the room, following the stone wall on my right.

Soon, a large fireplace came into view. Two gigantic wolves carved from marble stood ten feet apart, either side of the fireplace.

I felt a blast of cold air hiss of the gaping opening in the wall.

The townspeople weren't kidding. This was the coldest part of the castle, and in a frozen wasteland like Borzick I thought it couldn't get any colder. The drafts from the winds at the top of the castle caught in the chimney and came all the way down to the under-hall.

There probably hadn't been a fire in this fireplace for years.

I tried to hold up the lantern higher to see more of the stone and marble work. That's when I found it. The skull sat atop the mantel on the right side. Its perfect whiteness gleamed back at me through the darkness.

I quickly set down the lantern and began to climb up the right wolf. The fireplace must have been a good five or six feet high, but I made short work of it.

And then I had it. The skull had an unnaturally smooth surface.

"All this had better been worth it," I muttered as I reached into my pocket and pulled out a plain gold ring.

I took a quiet moment. For the last five years I had spent my evenings falling asleep while holding that ring, staring at it, longing for him – for my Tristani.

No more hesitation, I thought, and shoved the ring into the skull's hollow eye.

I spoke a few ancient words I didn't understand the meaning of, and instantly the skull's magic went to work. It shuddered in my grip before floating up in front of me. The ring inside the skull glowed with a dark hue before turning to mist. Like an early morning fog, the mist spilled out of the eye and engulfed the skull. Slowly the mist formed the shape of a body, a body I knew all so well.

Slowly the mist materialized, becoming solid flesh and bone.

There he stood immaculate, naked, his white skin perfect and glowing. My husband, Tristani. He was beautiful. Suddenly, it wasn't cold anymore, as if somehow the skull – or Tristani – warmed the area with magic.

For a moment, he caught his bearings. His pale orange eyes looked into mine. His face lit up.

"Dawni?" he whispered.

"Shh. We only have a little time together. Make me remember it forever."

I grabbed him and pulled him close before he could protest and kissed him deeply. I had dreamt of that sensation every day since he had died.

He lost himself in the moment with me. He pulled on my ratty, stained dress, lowering it off my shoulders. It quickly fell to the stone mantel and slid off onto the floor. He took a step back to look at me. My rosy skin felt warm as I stood there in nothing but a pair of silver silk panties. I had worn them just for him.

His penis sprang erect, and the room felt even warmer.

"Don't make me wait," I whispered.

He dropped to his knees and pulled the panties away from my body. He cast them aside and dove in, drinking from the wetness between my legs. I ran my fingers through his white hair, tossed my head back, and moaned. Almost as quickly as he had started, I experienced my first orgasm. Light ripples of pleasure moved through me.

I pushed him onto his back and knelt down. His eyes lit up as I crawled over him, breathing lightly on his penis. I stuck out my tongue and flicked it along his shaft.

He shivered and moaned in pleasure, just as he always had done when I did this.

I brought him in between my lips and moved my tongue in circles over his head. He grabbed my hair gently, guided me. I took him deep into my mouth, felt him tickle the back of my throat. He closed his eyes, tilted his head. I let him thrust gently – the way he always liked to do it – in and out of my mouth, moving deeper down my throat with each movement.

He groaned loudly with pleasure. I pulled back off his cock, and his semen sprayed onto my breasts. He smiled in his content way.

"We're not done yet," I cooed. I moved up and mounted him before he could lose his erection. His member easily slid inside me. His eyes rolled back as my warmth engulfed him.

"So wet," he said.

I nodded as I slowly thrust on top of him. "Touch me," I said.

He reached up and grabbed my breasts in his hands. The pleasure became more intense. I moaned and closed my eyes.

He thrust upward, penetrating to the deepest regions inside me, and I cried out. He sat up and brought my breasts to his face. He took my left nipple into his mouth and sucked on it. I screamed out as the orgasm hit me in a wave. He thrust into me, and the waves of pleasure continued. Finally, the orgasm ended.

"Did you cum?" he whispered.

I nodded, basking in the afterglow. I gasped lightly for air. "Your turn again."

He lay back on the mantel and pulled out of me. Leaning over him, I placed his penis between my sticky breasts. He thrust with a mad earnestness that only a husband knew. His penis glided easily between my breasts. I watched with a smile as his face twisted in pleasure.

Finally, he cried out our god's name as the semen sprayed onto my breasts, face, and onto his own chest.

I curled up next to him, and he held me in his arms.

We lay there for a moment, feeling the chill slowly return. Soon, he would be gone again and, just like last time, there would be nothing I could do about it.

I turned to him and whispered, "I love you."

He nodded, which meant he loved me too.

The cold became prevalent, and I could already feel his body weakening, turning to mist. "I'll find another way, a more permanent way to bring you back," I said.

"Don't leave me waiting for too long," he said. And then he was gone. All that remained were the perfectly white skull and a gold ring.

"There you are!" An angry voice cried from across the hall. Lord Farshaw stalked towards me with a lantern held high over his head. "You're going to wish you were dead when I'm done with you!" He screamed.

I leaped from the mantel and grabbed my dress and silk panties. Without another glance I leaped through the fireplace and up the chimney, climbing the blemishes in the rock towards the cold frosted sky above.

I had a new quest to start.

King and Queen

By Frank Sawielijew

"The emissary from the kingdom of Almyr, Your Divine Highness," the herald announced as the doors opened to admit her to the throne room. This had been easier – much easier – than she had expected. After weeks of preparation, all it really took were a few pleasant smiles and that magic twinkle in her eyes that made all men bend to her will.

Tarena dismissed the herald and the guards with a wave of her hand as she approached the king. Without so much as throwing a glance at their ruler, they left the room and closed the doors behind them. She was alone with the god-king of Lassûm, the most powerful ruler in this corner of the globe.

A playful smile appeared on her lips when she looked at him. Lašbalsummar, the glorious god-king, was strong willed and proud, a man worthy of the throne. But for Tarena, he was merely another challenge to test her skills against.

He got up from his throne, the golden discs hanging from his belt tinkling softly as he rose. "What brings you to my royal house, ambassador? I don't recall any messages from your king to announce your arrival."

Tarena fell to her knees, spread her arms, and kissed the ground – the traditional gesture of submissive adoration towards the god-king of Lassûm.

"I was sent to discuss matters of politics with you, o great god-king." The kingdom of Almyr was a neighbour of Lassûm and had good relations with Lašbalsummar. Tarena had researched his relationships to other rulers in detail and chosen a background for herself accordingly. "My king wishes to deepen the bond between our two nations, as there lie only benefits in friendship."

Lašbalsummar nodded and gestured for her to rise with an upward movement of his hands. "Very well. I shall open my ear to what you have to say. Rise, ambassador."

She got back to her feet and, for one short moment, her eyes met with his. They twinkled with that magical spark few men could resist, and she thought she saw a reaction beneath the curls of the god-king's long beard.

Could it be that even a god-king could fall to her charms?

She walked over to the heap of pillows in the throne room's corner, but Lašbalsummar commanded her to stop. "These pillows are reserved for myself and the women I bed. I haven't allowed you to seat yourself there, emissary."

So he hadn't fallen under her spell yet – but, she admitted, that would've been too easy. Weaker kings could be charmed with a single smile, but Lašbalsummar was a tougher nut to crack.

That, she thought, made him even more appealing. She turned around and showed him the sweetest smile her lips could conjure. "Please, your Divinity, I've walked many miles to get here and would like nothing more than to sit down and take my boots off to allow my feet some rest."

In the weeks and months before she travelled to his palace, she had tried to find out as much about Lašbalsummar as she could. As he tended to bed the noblewomen of the regions he conquered, information about his preferences had been easy to come by. She knew he had a love for feet and planned to use that to her advantage.

He stared at her with a look of both anger and respect in his piercing eyes. "Most others would've thrown themselves at my feet and apologized, but you... you ask for permission to do what I just forbade you? That is as foolish of you as it is brave, woman."

She bowed politely, then locked eyes with him and offered another smile. "I didn't wish to offend, Your Divine Highness. I merely wish to sit down and get my feet out of these boots after a long day of travel."

She kept her eyes locked with his, not allowing his gaze to intimidate her. He was used to women submitting to him without question – what could be more exciting to a man like him than one who would match his will rather than bend to it?

"Very well," he said. "Make yourself comfortable, woman. But know this is a privilege not granted to many."

She bowed again before turning around and seating herself among the pillows. She grinned to herself, barely able to repress a chuckle. *A privilege not granted to many* – she was pretty sure that meant *only to the women I sleep with.*

She unlaced her leather boots and slowly pulled them off her feet. Then, she propped her feet up on a pillow and wiggled her toes. Lašbalsummar watched her curiously. She sat there in a pose clearly meant to be seductive, her stockinged feet positioned so he could clearly see her soles, her fingers idly playing with a loose strand of her waist-long hair... even the long purple dress she wore was cut in a way that accentuated her feminine curves.

"You didn't come here to discuss politics, did you?" he asked.

"Why don't you sit down next to me and find out?" she asked back with a wink.

Lašbalsummar narrowed his eyes, but, after a moment of hesitation, walked over to the place of pillows. He might have been angry, but in his movements, there was a tension stemming not from anger alone. Her boldness not only enraged, but enthralled him. After a long moment, in which he just stared down at her with his penetrating eyes, he sat down.

She placed her feet on his lap without even asking for permission. He might have been a god-king, the ruler over hundreds of thousands of people, but in her hands, he was only a man – and she was a seductress with the power of magic at her disposal. It was a subtle magic, but powerful nonetheless.

"You're overstepping your bounds, woman," he said, his voice harsh with anger. But, Tarena noticed, there was also a hint of arousal in there.

She smiled and rubbed her feet against his thighs. "I didn't wish to offend you. Will there be punishment for my transgression, Your Divine Highness?"

"You weren't sent here by your king," Lašbalsummar said. "You came here on your own, because you wanted to meet me."

"Maybe." She smiled at him again, moving a hand to his face. His lip twitched when she ran her fingers through his beard, but he did nothing to stop her. "You're a handsome man, and you're a god. Why *wouldn't* I want to meet you?"

"You're bold, woman. It's infuriating, but for some reason, I *like* it." For a short moment, a smile danced across his lips, but it vanished as quickly as it had appeared. "But you should know your feet are treading on a dangerous path."

"If where I put my feet offends you, my lord," she said, "then please, guide them to a place more suitable."

She stretched her legs, moving her feet closer to Lašbalsummar's face. It was an obvious gesture that didn't fly past him.

The god-king laughed. "You're the most daring woman I've ever met, emissary – if you even *are* an emissary! You come here, act like you own this place, and try to seduce me in the crassest of ways. What do you expect from this?"

She poured most of the magic she had into one seductive smile, staring at him with her gleaming eyes that could melt hearts. "I expect you to take me, great god-king of Lassûm, conqueror of countless lands – and women. I wish to be one of your conquests."

For a long moment, he stared at her with his piercing eyes. Then, a rare grin appeared on his stern face. "Very well. Your bravery deserves to be rewarded. You shall have what you came for."

He grabbed one of her feet, lifted it up to his face and plunged her stocking-clad toes into his mouth. His other hand caressed her leg, slowly moving up to her thigh.

Tarena opened the clasp of his belt and let it slide down and disappear between the pillows. Pulling the fabric of his long embroidered tunic out of the way, she placed her hand between his legs.

She felt him harden under her touch and, with a grunt, he tore open her stocking to reveal her bare toes. His hands held her leg in a strong grip while he licked and sucked on her foot. Tarena loved the feeling of his tongue between her toes and expressed her enjoyment with a soft moan.

Her moan made him pause for a moment. Staring at her with eyes that disapproved of her merely sitting there and enjoying how he used her body, he said, "Don't just sit there, woman. Pleasure me."

"Of course, my king."

She pulled his pants down, placed her hand on his shaft and moved it up and down in a slow, steady rhythm. With each stroke he became harder, and his breathing became faster.

"Come closer," he ordered her. He released her leg, and she moved so close to him that she almost sat on his lap. He grabbed the front of her dress and tore it open, baring her breasts. They were small and firm, and he laid his hands on them as soon as he had pulled the torn cloth aside. Just as it had been with her foot, his play with her breasts was rough and aggressive. Her body was his to use, and his hands were those of a conqueror.

Usually, kings fell to their knees to please Tarena when she seduced them with her magic smiles, but Lašbalsummar, despite having fallen to her charms, was dominant. He did with her as he pleased, tore the clothing from her skin and ordered her to pleasure him.

It aroused her more than she had expected. A man like this, so strong of will, so unbending... she wanted him. She pulled off the undergarments below her skirt and got up, but Lašbalsummar grabbed her arm and roughly jerked her down again.

"You haven't earned your own pleasure yet," he said with the commanding voice of a conqueror.

"Yes, my king," Tarena responded, lowering her head. "I'm sorry."

She got on her knees and took him into her mouth. Her hand caressed his shaft again, gently massaging it while her tongue teased the tip of his cock. She was aroused by his dominance and glad to please him, but when he put a hand on her head to control the pace of her movements, she remembered that *she* was supposed to be the seducer, the controller, the dominant one.

She was here to make him fall under her spell, to seduce him until he was ready to share his riches with her. And she was determined to prove that she could control anyone with her charms, even a god-king.

She took him out of her mouth and pushed his hand away. "I don't need your direction to please you, my king. Let me work my magic on my own."

Tarena saw a short flash of anger in his face, but it vanished quickly, making way for a smile. Her fingers, still caressing his shaft, felt him throb with excitement. Her boldness aroused him as much as his dominance aroused her. "Very well, woman. Do your work."

Tarena put her lips on the tip of his cock again, teasing it with her tongue, while her fingertips stroked his shaft ever so lightly. Only when she noticed him tense with anticipation, she took him deeper into her mouth. *I am in control now*, she thought while her tongue circled around the tip of his cock, giving him only the hint of pleasure. *You are mine, god-king.*

Then, she sucked his cock in earnest, moving her lips up and down his shaft while she stroked its base with her fingers. Lašbalsummar moaned, and she slowed down again. Her tongue danced across his tip in a steady rhythm, licking up the juices that oozed from it.

Tarena knew he was ready to enter her. She didn't wait for his command – she took him out of her mouth, got up, and lowered herself onto his lap.

"You want me, my king," she whispered into his ear. "I can see it in your eyes."

"You didn't wait for my permission, woman," he said, but he didn't push her away when she guided his cock inside her with her hand.

"Yes," she said with a grin. "And I don't have to."

Before he could protest, she kissed him, and he let her. While their lips were locked in a sensual kiss, she began to ride him, slowly moving her hips back and forth. Lašbalsummar, god-king of Lassûm, had almost managed to dominate Tarena, seducer of kings, but now she was in control, just as she wanted to be.

She was on top of the proudest ruler in the world, and she had taken control of him with a simple kiss. When their lips separated, she put one hand on his shoulder and stroked his beard with the other.

"I love you, my great king," she said while she rode him.

"I want you to come for me. I want you to fill me with your divine seed."

She locked lips with him again, letting the magic flow through her blood to make the charm as effective as she could. With her arms wrapped around him, she rode on his lap, thrusting her hips hard and fast. She didn't stop kissing him even as his breath became heavier and his moans louder. And when she felt him come into her womb, she didn't stop moving her hips until the last drop of his seed was spent.

She placed one more kiss upon his lips before releasing him from her embrace and showing him a smile. Even as his erection subsided, she still kept him inside her. "Did you enjoy it, my king?"

"Enjoy it? Woman, you were wonderful."

"Thank you, my king." Now was the time to ask for a gift. Tarena traced a finger across his neck and fished out an amulet from below his tunic. It was a silver disc studded with three gems – a sapphire, a ruby, and an emerald. "This is beautiful. May I have it? A gift for the pleasure I gave you."

Lašbalsummar firmly shook his head. "A gift I shall gladly give you, but not this. I'll have my servants bring you something from the treasury. Something to match your beauty."

That surprised her. She knew she had him under her fingertips – he had fallen for her seductive charms, aided by the magic in her blood, as evidenced by his willingness to give her a valuable present. But why not this amulet?

"Oh, but I think it's really beautiful," she said with a sweet smile, putting all the magic she had left into it. "Don't you think it would suit me well?"

"It would." His voice became stronger again, as if her spells had no influence on him when he talked about the amulet. "But it was a gift, and I shall keep it close to my heart."

"A gift?" That was curious. Whose gift could be strong enough to break her magical charms? "Who gave it to you?"

"The Forest Queen." He chuckled when he saw the surprise in Tarena's eyes. "She gave it to me as a blessing when I promised to leave her lands alone. It's hard to believe, isn't it? A conquering god-king bowing his head before a creature of myth… "

"A creature of myth?"

He nodded. "The Forest Queen is the legendary ruler of the woodlands to the east. I hadn't believed the stories until I met her. I led an army into her lands, and – I don't even remember how it happened. I got lost on my own. Then I met her. She… no. Enough about that. Why am I telling you all this?"

The Forest Queen. Could it be she was a sorceress more powerful than Tarena? Or even something more than human? Her magic, at least, seemed to be stronger than anything Tarena could summon. What if she were to meet that woman? Would she be able to use her charms on her?

"I apologize for asking about things that don't concern me, my king," said Tarena.

Lašbalsummar waved it off, and his voice turned softer again. "Ah, it doesn't matter. You've given me great pleasure today, woman. I'll call my servants to bring you a new dress and some beautiful pieces of jewellery to adorn you."

"Thank you, my king. It has been an honour to make love to you."

He grinned. "And it has been a memorable experience for me, woman. A welcome change from the submissive women who fall to their knees and beg to please me. Now, get up and fetch a servant, will you?"

"As you wish, my king." Tarena got up from Lašbalsummar's lap, covered her breasts as well as she could with her torn dress, and went to the door.

***

Lašbalsummar, god-king of Lassûm, had given Tarena enough golden trinkets to buy a kingdom. Seducing him hadn't been easy, but now there was an even greater challenge before her. She had been riding for days, and finally her horse's hooves trod the ground of the expansive forests of the east. They were wild lands where no human settlements could be found for many miles.

She wanted to find the Forest Queen, and seduce her as she had seduced the greatest kings of human lands. To her, it was all a game, a set of challenges to be overcome. Ever since Tarena had discovered her magic talent, she had used it to charm kings and queens, lords and ladies, the rich and the powerful.

She had seduced a god-king. Soon, she would seduce a being of myth.

Even though she didn't know how to find the Forest Queen, she knew she'd meet her. She had known it from the moment Lašbalsummar mentioned her name. Somewhere within this beautiful forest, she would meet her.

After a while, Tarena dismounted and continued on foot, as the pathways became narrower and the ground more treacherous. As she walked through the forest, she realized how beautiful it was: the tall trees stretching their branches into the sky, the fragrant and colourful flowers adorning the ground. She wondered whether the Forest Queen was as beautiful as the land she ruled over.

Just as she thought about that mythical woman, a voice as soft as the song of birds addressed her, "Welcome to my realm, dear visitor. I greet you warmly."

Tarena turned around and saw the most beautiful woman she had ever laid eyes on. Her skin was as pale as the glow of moonlight on the still waters of a lake, her eyes as green as the leaves of ivy, her lips as red as cherries. Her body was covered only by her long auburn hair falling softly over her breasts and almost touching her knees.

"You're beautiful," Tarena said, stunned by the Forest Queen's beauty.

"Thank you," the woman responded with a smile. "What brings you to my lands?"

Tarena saw the magic in her smile. The Forest Queen was a seducer like herself, a woman who could win any heart if she tried. "I came because of the tales I heard about you, lady of the woods. A friend told me he met with you… "

"Your words flatter me, young woman. It is the forest that lends me my beauty. Do you like it here?"

"Yes, it's wonderful. So serene and peaceful… " Tarena looked around and took in her surroundings. Her booted feet stood on the soft wet grass of a glade, in the centre of which there was a small lake. *Strange*, she thought, *I thought I was still on a footpath through the forest.*

Again, there was a smile on the Forest Queen's lips. "Why are you wearing those heavy boots? Come, take them off and feel the grass beneath your soles! You shouldn't imprison your feet in these things."

Tarena nodded and sat down to unlace her boots. Why did she even wear them in a place like this? It was so much better to feel the soft earth and wet grass under her feet. She pulled them off, revealing one stockinged and one bare foot, as one of her stockings had been ripped by the god-king she'd seduced.

Seduced. She was here to seduce the Forest Queen. This was the perfect place for it. It was calm, beautiful, romantic.

What better place could there be?

"You must've walked a long way to get here. Let me massage your feet, it will help you relax," the Forest Queen said in her sweet, melodic voice.

"Yes, that would be nice. Thank you," Tarena replied, letting out a relaxed sigh as the Forest Queen's fingers rubbed the tension from her tired soles.

"Let me take your stockings off to make you more comfortable. One of them is torn, anyway... you don't need them anymore," the woman said as she pulled the stockings from Tarena's legs.

Tarena didn't mind. She closed her eyes and smiled when the Forest Queen put her fingers to her soles again. They sent waves of pleasure dancing from the bottom of her feet right up into her spine. It was almost magical.

Tarena opened her eyes again when she felt a wet tongue between her toes. "What are you doing?"

"Making you feel good." The Forest Queen smiled at Tarena with her cherry-red lips, her eyes sparkling in the sunlight. "Just lie down and relax."

Tarena had the feeling that something was going on, but she discarded the thought and closed her eyes again. The Forest Queen was right. She should just relax and enjoy the sweet, sweet touch of her tongue. She had never known something could feel that good on her feet. The Forest Queen's tongue danced upon her heels, then slowly moved along her soles and slipped into the spaces between her toes. A feeling of bliss went through her body, a feeling she usually felt only when...

"You're a beautiful woman," whispered the Forest Queen's sweet voice. "You shouldn't hide your body under so much cloth. Take off that dress so you can feel the sunlight caressing your skin, my sweet little darling."

Tarena's hands undid the laces of her dress almost unconsciously. Her mind was entirely focused on the touch of the hands upon her skin, soft hands, gentle hands, lovely hands that knew how to touch a woman. Those wonderful hands helped her undress, and finally her beautiful body was no longer hidden beneath a layer of cloth. She felt so free with the grass and the air and the sun touching her naked skin.

"I love you, oh lady of the woods, I love you... " she whispered, opening her eyes again to look into that lovely face in front of her. That lovely face, so close to her, so close... and then, a kiss, the Forest Queen's lips touching her own, a taste of sweet berries as she opened her mouth to return the kiss.

"Take me, my queen! I want to feel your touch upon my skin, your hands, your tongue... " A small part of Tarena wanted to resist the Forest Queen's charms, telling her that *she* was the one who should seduce and be in control, but she didn't care. She knew she had fallen for this lady of magic, and she wouldn't have wanted it any other way. It was such a different, such a refreshing experience to have another apply all the skills of seduction on her.

Now, she finally realized *why* her magic was so effective. She finally knew what it felt like to be charmed by a magical seducer.

The Forest Queen smelled of apples and flowers and her skin was soft as silk. Tarena moved her hands over her back, her arms, her shoulders, her breasts. The magical woman returned the favour, using her skilled hands to send one rush of pleasure after the other through Tarena's body.

Then, the Forest Queen's nimble fingers slipped between Tarena's legs, gently rubbing her womanhood. While her hand pleasured her down there, her tongue played with her breasts, lightly dancing around the nipples. It was enough to entice a soft moan from her.

And that was just the beginning. Skilfully, expertly, the Forest Queen pleasured Tarena, stimulating all the sensitive spots of her body – she rubbed her clit, gently bit her nipples, kissed her neck, let her fingers run along the skin of her arms and her legs, tickled the soles of her feet. Her touch made every inch on Tarena's body tingle with excitement.

But passively enjoying the Forest Queen's skills wasn't enough for her. When she looked at the Forest Queen, she wanted nothing more than to touch her, to smell her, to taste her, to explore that beautiful body with all her senses. "Please, let me love you, dear queen. I want you so much!"

The Forest Queen smiled, that sweet smile that could melt any heart, and placed a kiss on Tarena's lips. "You'll have me, then," she said, "and I'll have you."

She lay down next to Tarena, with her head at Tarena's feet, and licked her toes. Then, starting from the foot, she ran her tongue up Tarena's leg until she reached her womanhood.

Tarena smiled. *You'll have me, and I'll have you.* She put her face between the Forest Queen's legs and returned the favour. Slipping her tongue between the soft lips of her hot cleft, she tried to give the Forest Queen as much pleasure as she gave her.

For a long time they lay there, pleasuring each other with their mouths while their hands explored each other's bodies. The Forest Queen knew exactly how to use her tongue, and Tarena enjoyed every blessed moment of it. Even though she knew it was coming, the sudden surge of pleasure she felt was so intense, it took her by surprise. Her entire body exploded in a feeling of bliss that seemed to last for minutes.

When it subsided, she was left with a feeling of serenity, at peace with herself and the nature around her. "Thank you, my queen," she whispered.

The Forest Queen kissed her on the forehead. "It was my

pleasure." There was that wonderful, magical smile again. "But now, sleep, my dear. Sleep."

The Forest Queen's beautiful smile was the last thing Tarena saw before she fell into a deep slumber.

When she awoke from her peaceful sleep, she was no longer in the glade. The Forest Queen was gone, and so were all of Tarena's clothes and ornaments. What was left was that feeling of deep contentedness and the memory of the Forest Queen's gentle touch and beautiful smile.

When she got up, she discovered a small silver amulet in her hand, wrapped around her wrist with a silver chain. It was smaller and simpler than the one Lašbalsummar had worn, but it was clearly a gift from the Forest Queen. When she touched it, she didn't feel hard metal under her fingers, but the soft skin of that magical woman who had given her such great pleasure.

And she remembered the words she had heard in her dream.

"You came here to play a game, my dear," the Forest Queen had whispered into her ear. "So I played, too, and won. But I could feel how much you enjoyed it. I have a gift for you to remember me by."

She remembered a kiss after that, and sleeping in a bed of flowers, surrounded by beauty on all sides.

Now, she was back on the path that had taken her deeper into the Forest Queen's realm, exactly at the spot where she had left her horse.

Despite having lost everything she had won from Lašbalsummar, Tarena laughed. She had been defeated in her own game, and now she stood here, stark naked in the woods, with not even a shred of cloth left to her.

She had finally found her match, and surrendering to her skills had felt wonderful. She mounted her horse and, with a smile on her lips, rode back to civilization. She had been defeated, and yet it had been sweeter than any of her victories.

Her fingers touched the amulet that felt as soft as the Forest Queen's skin. *And my defeat won me a trophy more precious than any I have ever won in victory.*

The Olive Harvest

By Joanne Hall

Cassani lay awake and stared into the darkness, rigid as death. She watched the silver bars of moonlight inch their way across the floor, and silently cursed the gods for her ill fortune. Beside her, Spiradon snored. It was the only thing he did in bed these days.

It was hard to believe they had been married only two years. Two summers ago Spiradon had been as lustful as a drunken satyr, but as the olive harvest failed and they struggled to make the farm profitable, the fire had died within him. He was always too tired now. Too tired for lovemaking, often too tired even to talk to his wife.

Cassani felt herself withering away inside, like the trees in the orchard that bore no fruit, and the thought made her clench her teeth in frustration. She could not lie here all night next to this snoring pig, staring at the ceiling and wishing for something that would not happen. She would burn up if she didn't do something, catch fire and curl and blacken, twisting in the heat like an old dry tree.

A volley of barking from outside broke the spell of tension that held her, and she sprang out of bed, snatching up her shawl from the bedpost. As a precaution she grabbed Spiradon's stout axe, propped behind the kitchen door, before she let herself out into the night. These were wild times, and it was wise to be careful.

She drew her shawl tighter around her as the wind tried to whip it away. The farm was usually protected by the olive groves, but tonight the wind blew in from the west, blowing fresh off the sea and carrying the tang of salt and fish. Maybe the scents had upset the dog. Cassani lit the big storm lantern, and went to investigate.

Kou strained against his leash, scrabbling his front paws against the ground. One head twisted back over his shoulder at her approach, tongue lolling in greeting. His other two heads were firmly pointed towards the direction of the hills, black nostrils twitching in excitement. As she laid a hand on the back of his neck she felt every hair prickling. He whimpered as she unhooked the chain, and she was almost jerked off her feet by his eagerness to be away. She wrapped the end of the leash around her wrist and let him drag her in the direction he was barking. She had reached the low stone wall that marked the boundary of the farm when she heard the sound of hoof beats thrumming swiftly against the turf. A dark shape leapt over the wall and slammed into her shoulder, sending her sprawling. The chain tangled about her wrist as she fell, and she felt something crunch deep inside her arm.

Kou tore free, racing off into the darkness, baying from all three throats. Cassani tried to push to her feet, and a bolt of white-hot pain shot up her arm. She gagged, feeling her wrist twist unnaturally as she leaned her cautious weight on it, using her good hand and the wall to haul herself upright. The lantern had not gone out, and she held it up, leaning against the wall to stop herself from falling in a faint.

Beyond the circle of flickering flame she heard Kou, snarling low in his throat. That meant he had cornered something, held it pinned while he awaited her command to attack.

"Who's out there?" she called, forcing all her courage into her voice, fighting down the pain in her arm. "Speak, if you have a tongue!"

"Call your hound off!" a man's voice bellowed in reply. "I mean you no harm!"

Cassani couldn't hold the axe and the lantern at the same time. She propped the light up against the wall, retrieved the axe and hefted the weight of it. Whoever the stranger was, he'd best not try anything.

"Come here then, where I can see you!" She gave a low

whistle and Kou was by her side at once, quivering with anticipation, rumbling low in his chest. She quieted him with her hand.

A man emerged into the lantern light, bare-chested and densely bearded, riding a horse of the same colour. No, not riding, she realized, struggling to make sense of what she was seeing, through the haze of moonlight and lantern-light and pain. He was merged with his ride. A man-horse. A centaur. She hadn't seen one in these parts for many years. The stranger held up his arm to ward off the light. "What do you want?" Cassani demanded.

"I'm being hunted. I need a place to hide out for a few days. Please, my lady, I'll be no trouble."

Peering closer she could see blood on his arm, an arrow-graze. Kou licked his lips, drool gathering in long, sticky strings.

"Who's hunting you?"

"The hill-men." He gestured behind him to the dark shapes of the rocky hills. Cassani could see lanterns moving there, in the distance. "I wandered into their territory, and they set their dogs after me. They'll bore of the chase soon, but for tonight... "

All her judgment told her she should turn him away, not let this beast onto their property, that Spiradon would rage and panic if he knew she was letting a stranger, and worse, a half-man, through their gates. She slowly lowered the axe.

"You can stay for one night," she told him. "You sleep in the barn. I want you off my property by morning. Any tricks and I'll set the dog on you."

Kou belied his ferocity by wagging his tails and wiping drool on her bare leg with his closest head. She drew him close, wrapping her hand in the fur at the scruff of his neck, leaning on him for support.

"Follow me then," she told the centaur.

She could feel him walking behind her. It wasn't just the clop of his hooves, but the weight of his eyes on her back, making her tighten her grip on the handle of the axe. When she opened the barn door and ushered him inside, the velvet brush of his flank made her tingle all over in a way that wasn't entirely fearful. There was something about him, this dark-bearded stranger.

Kou growled, and she remembered herself, sending him back to the house with a gesture and a sharp word as the centaur turned back to her, brow furrowed in concern.

"Are you all right?" He laid a hand on her shoulder, fingers working into the fabric of the shawl. "Your wrist is broken. That's my fault, and I'm sorry. I can help you. Do you have light?"

She indicated the cold barn lantern with a nod of her head. Her wrist was throbbing now, waves of pain pulsing up and down her arm, and she wanted nothing more than to sit down. She forced herself to remain on her feet as the centaur ignited the lantern, casting light over the empty olive barn, clouded with cobwebs. A few dried-up husks crunched under her feet as, despite herself, she edged closer to the stranger.

"Allow me." The brush of the centaur's hand against her arms was unexpected, his fingers warm and calloused. She twitched away, and he took a polite step back. In the lamplight she could see him clearly for the first time.

He was taller than a human, and broader across the chest than most men she knew. The close-cropped hair on his head was the same dark brown as that of his glossy flanks, edging to black where his hair met his beard. His eyes were startling blue, and his generous mouth looked as if it would laugh readily, but at the moment it was downturned and serious.

"Your arm," he reminded her, reaching out once more.

Cassani realised she was staring, felt the flush in her face and over her chest. She nudged the shawl up over her shoulders, and held out her arm for him to study. His warm touch ran over her shattered wrist, and she felt a tingling sensation flow through the bone, driving out the pain.

"Is that better?"

She nodded, flexing her hand, conscious of his breath against her skin. Every inch of her felt alive, more alive than it had for months.

"It will be fragile for a time, but you will have no more pain." He let her hand go and stepped back, and she felt the gap open between them, cold and distant as the night sky. She wanted to step forward again, but she didn't know how.

"Thank you." She stared down at the dusty boards, nudging an olive husk with her bare toes, reluctant to meet his eyes. "I hope you'll be safe here. I'll make sure the hill-men don't find you."

"It's kind of you to shelter me."

He shifted his weight from one hind leg to the other, and a pained look crossed his face. She thought at first his scored arm was hurting him, but as he turned she saw the shaft of an arrow, snapped off and splintered, protruding from his right flank.

She reached out. The flesh around the wound was hot, and he shied away, one hoof striking instinctively against the barn floor. An echoing reminder, if any was needed, that he wasn't human. That he was unknown, and animal, and dangerous.

"Can I do anything... about that?" she asked. His flank was soft, but sticky with blood, and it had clumped together to render his hair into sharp little spikes.

"If you would." The centaur sounded relieved. "I could heal myself, but it's awkward to get the thing out. I don't have the reach. Could you do it for me?"

Cassani frowned. "I don't know," she admitted. "I don't want to hurt you… "

"If you leave it there, I will die. I hesitate to ask for your help once more, but you're the only one who can."

At this plea, she gritted her teeth and took hold of the broken arrow shaft. Offering up a quick prayer to Zeus, she wrenched it free. The centaur uttered a harsh cry of pain, a human cry, and lashed out with his hind leg, nearly catching Cassani on the knee. She jumped aside to avoid the blow. Blood was flowing freely down his flank, dripping onto the barn floor.

Cassani flung the arrowhead away and leapt to stem the sudden gush of blood with her shawl while the centaur bucked and twitched. "Hold still," she ordered him. "I didn't mean to hurt you. It's out now."

The centaur grimaced. "It will be better now it's gone," he said. "Will you help to heal the wound, as I healed your arm?"

"I don't know how."

"Take my hand, and lay your other hand on my flank." She did as he ordered. The blood ran hot beneath her palm.

"Now close your eyes."

Cassani felt a tremor burst through her, and she would have pulled away, if not for his reassuring grip on her hand. "Give yourself over to the feeling," he urged softly. "This won't hurt you, I swear."

His voice was so calm and steady that she felt herself relax, muscle by muscle. She allowed the healing energy to flow through her. She could feel the centaur's heart beating in his wrist, and her own heartbeat matching it, pulse for pulse. It was a feeling she had been missing for a long time, and she felt her breath quicken at the sensation, a rising that started in her chest and ran down her spine, a pulse beating hard between her legs. She groaned in pleasure, tightening her grip on the centaur's hand, longing to let the rising tide overwhelm her.

"Not yet." The centaur released her hand and stepped sideways, away from her, leaving her trembling and eager, frustrated on the brink of ecstasy. He hung his head. Beads of sweat stood out on his brow, and his chest heaved. "I'm sorry," he gasped. "I did not mean... for that to happen."

Cassani's body yearned for satisfaction, brimming with unfulfilled desire for so long, cheated at the last instant by his sudden withdrawal. She turned away, hiding her face, her sudden shame. "Nothing happened!" Her anger was more at herself than the centaur, for allowing herself to be tempted, drawn in and then rejected once again. "Nothing can happen. I have a husband, and nothing happens there either." Her lips snapped shut. She had revealed too much to this stranger, this beast.

He laid a tender hand on the back of her neck, light fingers stroking her hairline in a way that made her pulse quicken once more. "Why does nothing happen? Do you know?"

She felt hot tears of frustration sting her eyes, the well of eighteen months of failure full to overflowing. "The farm is failing," she said, her voice low and uneven. "The olives won't grow, and you can see the barn stands empty. Spiradon works every hour to try and save our livelihood, spends all his time worrying about it. He has no time, no strength left for me."

"Maybe I can help you?" The brush of his lips against the nape of her neck sent another powerful surge through her. "You have saved me. Let me stay here tonight, and tomorrow I will see what, if anything, I can do to save you." His mouth slid down to her throat, and she moved away quickly. The healing energy was one thing, but this was something more, and it was too much. Too fast.

"Listen, I don't even know your name." Did his kind even have names? "I don't think my husband would accept—"

"My name is Biryan. And I want to help you, and your husband. I want to save your farm, and your marriage. But you have to let me." He seemed to take her silence for assent. "Come to me here, tomorrow. My people have a gift for bringing life to barren places. I want to share it with you, my lady."

"Cassani. My name is Cassani. You are nothing but a beast. How can you help me?"

He stamped one hoof, in anger or denial, and at that sound the spell between them was broken. Cassani turned, fled into darkness, letting the barn door slam shut behind her.

***

Cassani could not explain why she did not mention the centaur to Spiradon, nor why, after he had left for town, announcing his intention to make an offering at the shrine of Demeter, she was irresistibly drawn back towards the olive barn. Her feet carried her there despite her will, and despite her misgivings. As she drew closer, circling, wary, she felt her pulse pick up speed once more. Twice her courage failed her and she turned back towards the house, and twice she found herself walking back towards the barn.

Biryan smiled as she pushed the door open and stood framed in the sunlight streaming in from the yard beyond. "I wasn't sure you would come," he said. "Will you walk with me under the trees, Cassani of the olive groves?"

It was a humid day, and the orchard offered a little shade. Cassani picked leaves off the stunted trees as they passed and watched them crumble between her fingers. The blight was spreading. Biryan swished his tail to keep the insects away as they walked, and Cassani laid a daring hand on his skin, on that strange join where man and horse merged. A finger on the horse, a finger on the man-flesh. He looked down at her hand and snorted with amusement, a very equine sound.

"What's it like?" she wondered aloud.

"As natural to me as being human to you. I have asked humans that question; they could no more answer it than I can."

"Have you known many humans?" By mutual, unspoken agreement they had come to a halt in a clearing. The grass grew long and thick here, but the trees above were almost nude. The branches should have bowed their heads beneath the weight of fruit at this time of year, the air filled with their scent. All Cassani could smell was sweat, horse sweat and human sweat. It wasn't unpleasant, but it was driving her wild, an itch she was desperate to scratch.

Biryan looked up at the barren trees, limbs stark against the sky. He shook his head, as if lost in thought.

"I have known a few humans, but I sense that's not what you're asking. Why not say what you're thinking, Cassani?"

"I was thinking of human women, and you... " She let her voice trail off. What was she thinking, asking such questions? "I'm sorry; it's none of my business." But the fire, in the barn... somehow that had made it her business. Even if nothing happened between them, she had to know whether or not it would have been possible. It would feed her fevered fantasies, while Spiradon lay inert beside her.

"Such a personal question!" Biryan laughed at her discomfort, not mocking, but kind. She felt that kindness in the brush of his hand over hers. "As you ask, yes I have."

"How?" She blurted out, belatedly realizing how rude she sounded. She snatched her hand away, distracted herself in a sudden intent study of the trees. "That is, I mean—"

He brayed with laughter. "It seems you're very interested, Cassani! Would you like to find out?"

Oh yes, by all the gods, yes! "I don't think it would be appropriate… "

"No?"

Before she could reply he had his arms around her waist and his mouth was pressing down on hers, searching, hungry. For a moment she resisted, and then she returned his embrace with the same fire, drawing his hand to her breast, shifting her weight until her nipple brushed against his palm. The thin fabric of her shirt between them, the threat of discovery – was that a footfall in the woods? They were out in the open, under the eyes of the gods themselves.

"We are all children of Zeus." It was as if he read her mind as he pressed closer, face buried in her neck, hands working unseen on the buttons of her shirt, at her waist, pushing her waistband down, parting her thighs, fingers sliding back and forth until she gasped. "He sees no sin in what we do. Why should you?"

"My husband," she protested, with no conviction. "He could come home—" The thought, the delicious transgression, made her hips shift harder against his hand.

"I know." Biryan folded his hind legs and collapsed into a half-sitting position, pushing her skirt to the ground. His lips brushed the warm skin of her belly when he spoke, tongue teasing around her navel. "Doesn't that excite you? It excites me."

Cassani was quivering all over, desire fighting with the fear of sin, fear of discovery. She hung back. "Biryan?"

"What's wrong?" He pulled her close again, strong fingers digging into the yielding flesh of her buttocks, mouth working over her torso.

She reached out tentatively. This couldn't happen. It couldn't *be* happening. "Half man, half horse. And, below the waist, all horse… "

Biryan held back a little. "Are you afraid, Cassani?"

"A little overwhelmed, perhaps… "

"You have no need to fear."

He was massaging between her legs again, slipping first one finger and then another deep inside her, making her gasp. "I would not hurt you," he said, into her hair. "But if you want me to stop—" He made to withdraw his probing fingers, and momentary panic seized her. She grabbed his hand, entwining her fingers with his as she pushed them inside her, guiding him, deeper in, and harder.

"The land and the people are one," he muttered, seemingly to himself. Responding to her urgent movements, he positioned her so her arms were wrapped around his waist, where he changed from man to horse. With one front leg on either side of her, he held her up, hands linked behind her back so her weight was supported on his forearms. And then, slowly and with great tenderness, he allowed her to slide down onto the hard length of him.

She gasped out loud as he slid inside her, and he froze, holding her up. "Is that too much?"

"No, oh no… " Cassani hardly dared to believe this was happening. Biryan leant back a little, steadying her with his arms and forelegs, allowing her to take control, letting her take him deeper inside her than any human could ever reach, unleashing fierce new sensations that made her cry out and dig her nails hard into the skin of his back, his flanks. It had never been like this with Spiradon, nor with any man. The sky, the trees, the gods themselves were spinning around her as she cried out, holding him tighter, losing herself utterly in the unexpected, long-awaited climax.

***

Cassani's shaking hands mirrored the flutter in the pit of her stomach as she prepared dinner. Spiradon had driven his cart through the gate an hour ago, but he had yet to show up at the house, and she was grateful for his absence. She had rinsed her hair under the pump, but she could still smell Biryan on her skin, scents of man and horse mingling with her own. She did not want to lose that smell, that memory. She ached from their lovemaking, and as she caught sight of herself in the glass she knew her eyes were suspiciously bright, her face flushed. She prayed to Zeus that Spiradon wouldn't notice.

The pump splashed in the yard, and Cassani hastily turned back to the stew she was preparing, hoping the steam from the cooking pot would be an excuse for the redness of her face. She heard Spiradon's soft tread on the flagstones as he slipped into the kitchen. He wrapped his arms around her waist and buried his face in her hair, inhaling deeply. She stiffened under the embrace. *What if he knows? What if he smells Biryan on me, and guesses? What will he do then?*

Spiradon plucked a piece of meat from her ladle and she slapped his hand playfully, keeping up the pretence. "Any luck at the shrine?" she asked. "Did Demeter show herself?"

"She did, for a change. I was lucky; I got to speak to her in person. She said something about the land and the people being one. I don't know—what?" She could not hold back her gasp at hearing Biryan's exact words repeated so soon, and by her husband. Did he know? How could he know? Maybe Demeter had told him. "Does it mean something to you?"

"I burnt my finger, that's all," she lied. "You shouldn't distract me." She turned to face him, her back pressed to the stove. He was so close she could see her reflection in his dark eyes, and she reached up without thinking to flick a dried-up olive husk out of his hair. He wrapped his arms around her, pulling her close, lips seeking hers. His hands worked over her breasts and she froze, caught by surprise, and fear.

"What's the matter?" Spiradon ran his thumbs over her hips. "Come on, we haven't done it for so long… "

"Why are you in such a mood?" She held him off, one hand against his chest, as he reached for her.

"Demeter herself spoke to me! I'm sure the harvest will be fine now—"

"It won't be fine, Spira! There's no fruit on the trees. There's nothing to harvest. The farm is barren. It's over!" She pushed past him, suddenly angry, and afraid. What had Demeter really said?

"Where are you going? Cass?"

"To have a wash. Leave me alone!"

***

She spent a sticky, sleepless night, restless in her desire for Biryan. Nothing seemed to matter but his touch, and she practically pushed Spiradon out of the door as soon as dawn broke. Whatever he had done to her she wanted, needed, more of it, husband and gods be cursed.

She dressed with trembling fingers, leaving her top button undone, allowing her blouse to fall open provocatively. She rushed through her household tasks, aware they had to be done, that she had to give at least the impression of normalcy. But the stranger in the olive barn called to her, and it was only an hour after Spiradon had left that she found herself walking across the arid fields once more, skin tingling, heart beating fast.

She pushed open the barn door without knocking, and slipped inside. She had expected to find Biryan waiting for her. She had expected to find him alone.

Spiradon crouched, on hands and knees, head thrown

back to expose the long tan curve of his throat. His eyes were closed, his lips trembling as he gasped and moaned. Biryan stood over him, thrusting rhythmically, calmly. The centaur looked around at Cassani's gasp, and his smile was benign even as Spiradon groaned beneath him.

"The land and the people are one," Biryan said, in a low voice. "I serve the Goddess Demeter. Will you stay and serve her too?"

"I... I don't know!" Her initial shock had receded a little, and now she stared in fascination as the centaur made love to her husband. She watched them moving together in the shafts of dusty sunlight that streamed through the high, narrow windows and felt once again the stirring of her own arousal. She was barely conscious of her movements as she pushed her hand down beneath the waistband of her skirt, slipping her fingers between her legs, surprised at how wet, how eager, she already was. She leant back against the wall, fingers shifting, never once taking her eyes from her husband and the centaur. Biryan caught her eye, and her movements, her rising lust, seemed to stimulate him to push deeper into Spiradon, quicker and harder. Her urgent fingers swiftly picked up the rhythm and matched him, thrust for thrust, until Biryan cried out, and Spiradon groaned and pitched forward, face down in the straw, with Biryan still moving slowly inside him.

The centaur was breathing heavily as he turned to Cassani and beckoned her over. She felt unsteady on her feet as he kissed her, darting his tongue in and out of her mouth. He tasted, she realized, like her husband.

"Lie down," Biryan told her.

"Where?" Was he going to take her on the barn floor, next to Spiradon?

Biryan lifted Spiradon up in his strong arms. His head lolled, and Cassani wondered for an instant if he had fainted. Biryan held the olive farmer him against his chest. "With your husband," he said.

She could see what the centaur meant now. She slipped between his forelegs, her head between his hooves, looking up into both of their faces. She would not question him. Whatever was going on here, whatever sin, whatever magic, she needed to be part of it, needed it in a way she understood only at the most primal level.

Spiradon's dark curly head rested against Biryan's tan shoulder as his mouth eagerly sought the centaur's. His eyes flickered open, and he started, appeared to notice her for the first time.

"Cassani! What are you doing here? This isn't—"

"Shhh." She didn't want him to tell her this wasn't what it looked like. She wanted it to be exactly what it looked like, her husband and her beast-lover coupling on the barn floor. She wanted to make him cry out the way Biryan had.

She raised her damp, salt-tasting fingers to his lips, and he sucked them like an infant at the breast. Spiradon was still hard, and as Biryan let him slip out of his arms Cassani reached for him eagerly, drawing him inside her with one hand on his backside and the other wrapped around Biryan's shaft. The centaur was moving again, above them both this time, and his every thrust against Spiradon drove him deeper into Cassani, until she cried out again and again, arching her back as wave after wave rippled through her muscles and her fists clenched and unclenched on the dusty floor.

And then the centaur was gone, slipping away without a word, not even a goodbye, leaving Cassani and her husband spent, wrapped around each other on the floor of the barn.

Outside, the olive orchard burst into bloom.

Cleopticus and Haerne

By Steven C. Davis

Cleopticus – Clop to his friends, not that he had any – stood before the tribute wall and the gate to the Golden Garden. The tribute wall, the Golden Garden, and more importantly the horror that lay within the garden had filled his young life with dread.

The chance of being chosen from the City of The Green and Grey, one of the seven cities that surrounded the Golden Garden, was not so great. One youth a year, to appease the creature in the Golden Garden, taken in turns by each city. One youth a year was fed to the creature. There were, collegiate estimates proclaimed, a hundred thousand in the city. Even broken down into families, and his tri-parent family with two elder sisters was not unusual: still, that was only about sixteen thousand choices. But both his elder sisters had passed through the choosing, and it was said the creature preferred males. Include the bias because his sisters had not been chosen – and Cleopticus hated them, and not merely for the fact they had not been chosen – and his selection had acquired a certain inevitability.

The wall was gently curving golden bricks, bound with an unbreakable mortar, sloping off to either side. To the left, some five miles distant, was the entrance from the City of Lilac Hues. To the right, some mere four miles distant, but over a considerably rockier path, lay the entrance from the City of Magenta Shadows.

Towering up over them, overshadowing them yet it cast barely a shadow, was the Golden Garden. Its circumference had never been accurately recorded. Some said the creature within, when not partaking of youths, remained near the wall, and did not like its cage to be measured. Others claimed there were guardians in the Golden Garden, who appeased the creature, and saw to it that no accurate measurement of the garden was ever made, lest the Seven

Cities decided to invade, to face the creature headlong once and for all. Still others, furtive types who drank in taverns and spoke too loudly when intoxicated, claimed the cities themselves did not want the true size of the garden revealed – but those that claimed this, did not elaborate why it might be so, and their declarations were often followed by drunken statements of love and devotion.

It smelled of grass and straw and hay. It smelled of trees, of orchards, of pollinating bees. It smelled ripe, fertile, and Clop was faintly uneasy.

In the centre, the highest point of the Golden Garden, grew a tree like no other, or possibly several trees. It sprang from the high, dry, centre of the garden, but there was no trunk. Rather, a multiplicity of trunks sprang from the central mound, and from each sprang more branches, some bearing fruit of monstrous size, it was claimed. The creature within, whom the Seven Cities sacrificed a youth to each year, ate such fruit. Or maybe guarded it, not that there ever had been any trespassers.

Cleopticus laid his hand upon the gate. It was golden green and coarse, metallic, rusted but not actually ruined to the touch. It did not swing open. That was another marvel of the Golden Garden. The walls were too high to climb. The gates sealed the garden in from the cities. A vacuum, a pocket, a world all of its own for the creature to roam. The creature that must never be loosed upon the cities, or they would fall.

Cleopticus shivered. Not that he was cold. Excitement and fear shook his body. None of the youths who had gone before him had ever returned. But in the millennia which the creature had lived – the Golden Garden should be littered with bones and rotten with decomposing flesh.

Maybe it was. The Golden Garden was unknown. Unexplored. It might well be death, but death was better than living with his sisters' actions. And his actions, his sacrifice, would absolve the guilt and shame he felt and render their subsequent conquests meaningless. There was pleasure in knowing they would be forever in his shadow because of his actions, his sacrifice.

Cleopticus removed his hand from the gate, crumbling flakes of metal between his fingers. He could smell the gate now, cold metal and rust, but rust so deeply buried, held together…

There was pressure on the gates, he realised. The wall was too high, too perfect, unbroken, but the gates, they were the weak spots. Pressure between the Golden Garden and the Seven Cities weighed upon the gates, creaking and crumbling them, twisting them in upon themselves, rusting to nothing until all that was left—

There was no gate. There was an opening, an entrance, an entry, into the Golden Garden. Wind rushed through it, pressure released, the scent of trees and rutting and deep, dark woodlands all intermingled. Cleopticus knew that he could stand there, and the wind would rush out of the Golden Garden. It would rush through him, and it would continue to rush until it wore down his resolve or until something – the creature within – found the opening, found him, and then found the City of The Green and Grey. He took a step forwards, feet upon the bottom of the gate that simultaneously was not there, and was there. The gate formed and dissolved, aware of him, the cold, rusted metal never actually touching his body but continually refreshing itself, trying to reseal the breach in the wall.

The wind that was and was not tore through him and around him. He had never felt anything like it. But then he had only lived sixteen years in the City of The Green and Grey, and he, a boy child – what experience had he to measure the wonders and strangeness of the Golden Garden against?

Cleopticus crossed the boundary into the Golden Garden. The air was still. He could hear insects buzzing. The grass was soft, warm, and delicately moist to the touch. He knelt;

it was soft beneath his knees, beneath his pale skin. Some thought too fleeting to be caught, to even be aware of, made him raise his hands to his hairless cheeks. Not a man, not a boy, but a sacrifice, the price of the city's survival.

He ran fingertips down his throat. Down to his narrow shoulders and bony arms. He was not large, would not provide a meal for the creature if it was hungry. A snack. The thought almost made his lips twitch in amusement.

The grass rippled slowly, though he could feel no wind upon his face. It caressed the lips at the entrance to his body. His nipples stiffened. The feel of the grass, so soft, so gentle, elicited something he had not felt there for a while. Well, not without shame at least, and there was no shame in this.

Cleopticus closed his eyes. The grass – maybe it moved more to a measured heartbeat than a breath of wind – continued to softly caress his body at that most sensitive, intensive part.

He trembled softly. It was wrong. It was beautiful. It could not be wrong. He slid his hands along his thighs to his knees, leaning forwards ever so slightly. He had no fear of the creature.

Cleopticus bit his lip slowly, straining towards the hill at the centre of the Golden Garden, the peak, straining towards release. His back prickled with sweat. His palms were slippery. He bit deeper into his lip, trying to be silent, trying not to draw attention, but unable to contain his excitement.

He came, releasing only a single gasp to break the quietude. A single drop of blood from his lip fell to the grass. He tumbled forward, laughing, sprawling in the warm grass, looking up at the sky overhead. He could see the sun through the trees.

There were no trees. He was in a soft meadow, gently inclining upwards and tapering off to either side as it followed the circular wall. There were trees on the mound at the very centre of the Golden Garden and their branches, their shade, extended to cover the whole garden.

The sky had never looked so blue. Of course, the City of the Green and Grey had nothing to compare the blueness and the golden of the sun, which gave the garden its name.

Cleopticus lifted his head. Something was different. He wriggled over onto his stomach. Something was amiss.

The meadow still rose towards the mound at the centre of the Golden Garden, the brow of the hill. But there was an intemperate note in the wind which caressed his flanks and bottom. The sky was still as blue, but it was as if viewed through a lens, distorted and slightly ruffled. And the burning gold yellow of the sun – the burning gold was there, but it was pulsing, pulsing, pulsing.

Beneath, his feet the grass surged, echoed, rippled. The bees' buzzing became a discordant drone.

He looked back, half expecting to see no gate, but there was the gate. Exit, flight, betrayal would be possible, but it was not Cleopticus's way. What little he knew of himself and his capabilities told him it was not his way. He got to his feet, brushing grass from his body, his fingers damp from making himself presentable. He might be only a boy, but he was the elected one.

He took halting steps up towards the mound, up towards the source of the canopy which covered the Golden Garden, for surely there he would find the creature to which he had been sacrificed.

And then there the creature was, between him and the way onwards and upwards.

The creature had clear blue eyes. If the Golden Garden, with the mount at its high centre and the spreading canopy of branches, was the macrocosm, then she was the microcosm.

He had no sense of fear. By his decease, his city would survive another seven years. By his act, his sisters would be put to shame. Death was – interesting looking.

Death was female. He had seen females and unclothed females before; his sisters were, at least biologically, female. But this female creature was unlike any female creature he had seen before.

Was she part of the Golden Garden? Part, made manifest? Or was she an inhabitant of the Golden Garden, trapped there to prevent some terrible occurrence happening? Appeased, to prevent her leaving and wrecking terrible vengeance and destruction upon all seven of the cities.

It seemed a little farfetched.

A tale grown in the telling, perhaps.

Cleopticus drew himself up. He was not tall, he was not well built, but he was aware of his importance.

Her skin tone was not as pale, as albino-like, as his. After all, she was as naked as he but he was normally clothed. If this was her solitary habitat, she had no need for clothes.

She was... Cleopticus trembled slightly. He was aware of himself. The Golden Garden was, no doubt, aware of him. And if she was linked to the Golden Garden then by extension she would be aware of him. The musk in the air was his scent, his pleasure. He walked towards her slowly, the trembling easing.

She looked humanoid. But to compare her to the harpies of his sisters would be to compare a mountain filling half the sky to a mole hill. His sisters... he shuddered, repressing the memory.

The woman walked slowly, at ease. Her skin was pure and blemish free, glowing with vitality. Her hair was dark brown.

Rising from her head or her hair, he knew not exactly which, were branches without number, separating, sub-dividing, covering an area far beyond her body. The branches of her head hung heavy with fruit, ripe-looking golden apples.

She was not what he had imagined; slim, beautiful, exotic, strange, fearsome but not unpleasant to gaze upon. Her breasts were attractive and Cleopticus wondered for an instant what it would be like to be allowed to touch her there. Her nipples were small, the aureoles tight, each a shade darker than the encompassing skin.

He licked his lips. She was large, larger than any female he had seen. Her life-giving appendage was bifurcated at the end, the whole length ridged like bark and indeed flourished with small leaves and buds. Cleopticus swallowed awkwardly.

The shadow of her branches covered him. She approached, turning his side to her so that her appendage, erect and hardy, pressed against his stomach. Her hand caressed his bottom, and she stood close enough that he could feel her breasts against his arm.

"I can smell your pleasure, city boy," she breathed. Her fingers stroked between his cheeks. "There are not many who stand their ground before me."

Cleopticus didn't answer. He wanted to stroke, to touch her, but to do that would mean turning to face her. Doing that… She is the beast, the creature, he rationalised. Why am I afraid now. I did not run in fear. I will not stand in fear now.

He turned, and she let him. He raised his hands to her soft, warm, breasts, fingers teasing her nipples. He trembled.

"Touch my apples," she said.

He frowned, uncertain.

"The fruit which blossoms from my branches."

Reluctantly, he lifted his hands to the golden apples in her branches. They were ripe, firm, warm, even. She had tilted her head to watch and smiled.

Her hands were on his bottom, lifting, and then Cleopticus gasped as she penetrated him. She was broader than he had realised and rough, like a tree branch thrusting into him.

He cried out, but she was moving, leading him to the warm grass. The wondrous, terrifying, creature was sitting astride him, thrusting in long, slow, and hard movements.

Cleopticus gasped, wriggling and panting. He had never felt anything like it. Her bifurcated organ separated, and he cried out in ecstasy, thrusting hands outward, his feet slipping on the grass.

He threw his head back, climaxing, but she didn't stop. Her hands on his hips, built up a rhythm. Her member filled him, branches separating out, growing, moving independently, heading for his womb.

He reached out desperately, wanting to paw at her breasts, wanting to sink fingers into something soft and hold on as her appendage grew and thrust branches deeper into him.

Cleopticus screamed, climaxing again, but that only drove her to greater thrusts and a faster rhythm. He fell back, twisting this way and that, drained, empty. Then he felt her branches penetrate his womb and he orgasmed at the feel and the thought of her branches so deep inside him. She thrust once more, and it felt as if all his bones would break as her essence poured into him, filling his womb with tiny buds, and then he collapsed into unconsciousness.

***

Cleopticus opened his eyes slowly, feeling unaccountably warm and secure. He lifted his head from the pillow – the monster of the Golden Garden smiled tenderly at him. He became aware his body was heavy, not as he remembered, gravid.

"How long," he ran his hand over his swollen stomach. "How long was I – asleep?"

"Three months." She smiled beautifully. "You are the first man child who has been able to carry a child, even this far, in millennia."

Her arms were around him. Her appendage was quiescent. The halo of branches sheltering him was rather smaller than he remembered. He lay in possibly the same field he had passed through all those months ago.

"What...what am I?" he asked.

She smiled. "You carry the future. I will give you my strength, that the child will be strong within you."

She turned him in towards her, and his questing lips found her nipple. Milk and sap flowed, and Cleopticus felt the vitality flowing through him. He sat up. A teardrop of milky green stained her nipple. If anything, her branches looked even more diminished.

"Will you be here, when my child... " he trailed off.

She nodded, weakly. "As your child grows stronger, I will grow weaker. There will only be a short period of time when two of us exist in this world."

"What... who... what name are you given?" he settled on.

"Haerne." She smiled. "Your child will become the tree of the Golden Garden." She caressed his stomach. "My child." Her hand slid down below his belly.

Cleopticus was embarrassed to see the lips at the entrance to his body were crowned with fur. Her fingers parted his lips, stroking him gently. He bit his lip. His nipples stiffened. Goosebumps formed on his arms. Sweat touched his brow.

"You could not take a second penetration by the tree. Lie back."

Cleopticus lay back in the warm, pseudo-sentient grass. She knelt before him, her branches angling backwards so as not to scratch him, lowering her head to his hips. Her tongue licked them, and he felt as if his insides were turned to warm honey. He clutched at the grass, spreading his legs, raising his knees, sinking his heels in. She licked, applying pressure to his sensitive spot. Cleopticus gasped, climaxing, feeling his pleasure bubble over. Haerne stayed there, lapping at him, drinking, until he had no more to give.

She crawled up him, pausing to kiss his nipple before laying her head on his shoulder. He wrapped arms around her tight – her branches were diminishing, would soon be gone – and she slept in his arms. In his womb, her child grew, and nothing else mattered now to Cleopticus.

Camelot Girls Gone Wild

By Cheryl Morgan

“**S**o do you want be part of this orgy or not?” asked Isabelle.

Frida blushed pinkly, which suited her blonde complexion and powder-blue dress but quickly became boring when you did it as often as the Anglish girl did.

“Of course I do. I just wanted to make sure that you have the right spell. Greek isn’t exactly your strongest subject. Also, what happens if this satyr thing turns out to be dangerous? Have we thought about that?”

“If it is dangerous,” said Aiofe, “I happen to have brought my sword and will happily slice its cock off to protect you two delicate ladies.”

“You take your sword everywhere with you, even to bed,” noted Isabelle, accurately. “Quite how you think that is going to win you a husband is beyond me.”

“How about I find one I like, beat him up, and carry him off home?”

Isabelle wasn’t sure that the fiery, red-haired Irish girl was being entirely serious, but on reflection suspected that she probably was.

“Is that one of your traditional Irish mating customs, or have you just been spending too much time with that Hyrkanian sword mistress the school has employed?”

Aiofe shrugged. “It’s how most of our men approach mating. Which is not exactly ideal, but explain to me again how I am going to impress a knight with my skill at flower arranging, the way you plan to.”

“For goodness sake, stop arguing,” said Frida. “I want to

have time for a decent night's sleep when this is all over. Sex is supposed to be tiring, isn't it?"

"You mean you don't know?" asked Isabelle, raising a perfectly shaped eyebrow.

"As if you would," said Aiofe.

"Bitch!"

"Cow!"

"Shut up, and get on with it!"

"Well then," said Isabelle, "seeing as your Greek is so much better than mine, why don't you read the spell. Here."

The French girl dug into her bag and handed over a scroll. Frida blushed, again, but realized that she had talked her way into this one. Slowly but confidently, she began to read.

The woodland glade that the girls had selected for their adventure was lit solely by the light of the moon shining down through the circle of ancient oaks that surrounded it. Although dawn was a long way off, a faint mist began to rise off the grass. Mushrooms on the fallen boughs started to glow. The hunting bats which, had the girls been looking, would have been seen rushing around the crowns of the trees, suddenly made themselves scarce.

With the mist, a smell rose in the clearing. Part of it was clearly that of red wine, but underneath that was a note the girls were unfamiliar with. It was the distinct, strong smell of semen.

"Well hello, me lovelies, what can I be doing for you?"

The creature that wandered into the glade was somewhat taller than the girls had expected, but rail thin. He wore a straggly goatee beard, and through his shock of dark hair two short horns could be seen peeking. His chest was bare and hairless, but his lower body and legs were covered with thick fur and ended in neat little hooves.

His cock was disappointingly small and as limp as his wrist.

Isabelle, as was her wont, decided to take charge.

"I am the Princess Isabelle, daughter of King Benoît of Brocéliande. I, with the aid of my friends, have summoned you here."

"I'm Princess Aiofe, daughter of King Cormac of Tara," added the Irish girl, "and, yeah, we've summoned you."

"I am Princess Frida," squeaked the third girl, "and my father is Guthrum, King of the Angles."

"We are all," added Isabelle, "graduates of Morgan le Fay's School for Sorcery."

"Students actually," whispered Frida, who had a thing about honesty.

"Oh ho. Three young girls whose fathers have been beaten in battle by Arthur. Hostages, by any chance? Does Arthur know you are learning magic, I wonder?"

"Less of your lip, mythical beast," said Isabelle, still trying to exert her authority. "We didn't summon you here for you to insult our fathers."

"Ooo, who are you calling mythical?" asked the satyr. "I suppose you look normal enough, but your friends have really weird coloured hair. Do they dye it or something?"

"NO!" replied Aiofe and Frida in unison.

"They come from barbarian countries at the edge of the known world," said Isabelle, patting her luxurious dark curls. "It is nice to know that you appreciate good looks, Sir satyr."

"Well I do, my dear, but not exactly yours, if you get what I mean."

Aiofe and Frida giggled.

"No I do not. Explain yourself, creature!"

"How good are you at Greek, girly?"

Frida and Isabelle glared at each other.

"And what is that supposed to imply?" asked Aiofe, easing her sword out of its scabbard.

"Well," said the satyr, "my people come in two types. Not male and female, like you humans, but more divided by our tastes. Were you, by any chance, hoping for a bit of rumpy-pumpy on this fair night?"

This time all three girls blushed.

"I see from your reaction that my guess was correct. I am sorry to inform you ladies that, fair as you may be, you have got entirely the wrong faun. There are those among us, 'tis true, whose taste for the fair sex knows no bounds, and who would have been happy to keep all three of you entertained all night. The spell that you read so prettily, on the other hand, is for summoning one such as myself, whose amorous tastes lie in an entirely different direction."

"You mean you're gay?" asked Isabelle in disbelief.

"That would explain the thoroughly disappointing appearance of his cock," said Aoife, putting her sword away.

"I told you we should have checked that spell more carefully", said Frida.

"You read it," said Isabelle. "I bet you just pronounced it wrong."

"I'm afraid not," said the satyr. "The two words are quite

different. Your pasty-haired friend is entirely blameless in this respect."

"See, it's all your fault. Again."

"So much for collective responsibility," said Isabelle. "But there has to be some way to rescue this. We have our satyr, we know what turns him on, all we need is some means of helping him get it up. Now, who do we have here who might be mistaken for a man?"

"You want that pretty French throat of yours slit?" asked Aiofe, producing a very sharp looking dagger from her boot.

"OK, sorry, sorry. I was out of order... "

"I could read to him," suggested Frida.

"You could WHAT???"

"Wait," said Aiofe. "That's genius! You mean your fanfic, don't you Frida? Do you have some with you?"

"Of course, you never know when you might get time to write." Frida dug into her bag and pulled out a scroll.

"And what, pray tell," asked the satyr, "is fanfic?"

"Oh," said Frida, "it is short for fan fiction. A lot of us girls do it. We are all big fans of Arthur's knights, and we write stories about them. The most popular type of story is a romance between two knights. We call it *slash* because you categorise the stories by the pairing featured. This is one of the most common pairings, Galahad/Perceval."

"You mean you write gay porn?" asked the satyr.

"Well," replied Frida, warming to her subject, "I wouldn't exactly put it like that. It's more romance, you know, more cultured, subtle."

"But with fucking?"

"There's lots of kissing."

"Sounds a bit dull to me, but I might be interested. Tell me about these two knights."

"You mean you don't know about Galahad?" asked Frida. "He's a total dreamboat. All of the girls at school are madly in love with him. He's the youngest person to make knight in, like, forever. And he has the most gorgeous blonde curls. His hair is almost the same colour as mine," she preened.

"Go on," said the satyr, looking unimpressed.

"And then there's Perceval," added Isabelle, "who is like all dark and broody. The strong, silent type. He's always going off on missions on his own. We think he's harbouring some dark secret. Perhaps a childhood sweetheart who has been kidnapped by a wicked witch. Something like that. He's always training too. Not big and brutish like Gawain, but really strong and wiry. I bet he's got a lot of stamina."

"Success!" squeaked Aiofe.

"What?"

"His cock moved. I saw it!"

"This Perceval does sound interesting," said the satyr. "Tell me more."

"Shush!"

"What's the matter, Frida?"

"I heard something."

"She's right," said Aiofe. "Horse harness. Two of them I think. Someone is coming. We'd better hide."

The three princesses scooped up the trains of their ballgowns and scurried behind a nearby oak, where they were quickly joined by the satyr.

"If only some of my brothers could see me now," he said, nestling down between the girls. "They would be so jealous. Who makes your dresses dear, that's some really nice embroidery work."

"Shush! All of you."

Soon after two large warhorses entered the clearing. They were unarmoured, as were the young men who rode them, but from their dress and weapons these lads were clearly knights. In any case, the heraldry on their clothing gave the game away. One bore the red shield and black raven, the badge of Sir Perceval. The other bore a badge of a golden sun on a blue field, the colour of his badge perfectly matching his crown of golden hair.

"Galahad... " sighed all three girls in unison.

The collective sigh of feminine desire that they uttered was so heartfelt that it woke fair Titania far away in her leafy bower in the wild wood. As Oberon was in a drunken stupor, she summoned the young men of faerie to her, and kept them busy until morning.

"Nice little place you have found here, Perce," said Galahad as he dismounted.

"Thanks Gal. I was quite pleased with it. It is nice and quiet anyway. We'll be safe here. The last thing we want is someone finding out about us and that bully Gawain starting on. I can just imagine the 'real men' crap he'd come out with."

So saying, Perceval put one arm around Galahad's shoulder and with his other hand cupped the younger man's chin. Soon they were engaged in a passionate kiss.

"Oh my... " breathed Frida, feeling something push against her leg.

"Maeve's titties," whispered Aiofe, "that's one impressive weapon."

Isabelle's eyes were like saucers. She reached out a beautifully manicured hand to stroke the enormous penis that now sprouted proudly from between the satyr's legs.

Slap!

"Hands off girly," said the satyr, "that's not for the likes of you."

So saying, he stood up and, with hand on hip, began to stride into the clearing.

"Wait, they'll see us," whispered Aoife.

"Come back here, you lust-craved lunatic," said Isabelle.

"Don't interrupt them, I'm taking notes," wailed Frida.

But it was too late.

"Good evening, gentlemen. It looks like you are set on a good time this evening. Would you care for a threesome?"

"God's wounds," said Galahad, who was in the process of unlacing his codpiece. "You put us both to shame, Sir!"

"Aye," said Perceval, "I'd heard that some of your kind swung my way, but I'd never quite understood the attraction until now."

"I take it we have a deal, then," said the satyr, magically producing a flagon of wine from that mysterious alternate dimension created especially for his kind by Dionysius. "Cheers to that, I say."

He took a long swig, then indicated behind him. "Of course you lads had better sort something out with the little ladies first."

The three princesses, realizing that the game was up, stood and walked forward. Isabelle and Frida frantically brushed twigs and moss from their dresses while Aiofe did her best to make it seem like sleeping rough in the woods was something she did all the time.

"This evening is full of wonders," said Galahad. "To what do we owe the honour of the presence of such a bevy of beauties?"

"They were trying to summon one of my brothers for a night of rumpy-pumpy," said the satyr, "but they seem to have suffered a teeny spell malfunction."

"Oh my," said Galahad, trying not to laugh, "that does sound unfortunate. But I'm sure our knightly vows cover such eventualities. Am I right, Perce?"

Perceval did not answer. His mouth was full of the satyr's magnificent member.

"I'm glad it's him doing that," said Aiofe, "I don't think my mouth is big enough."

Isabelle was so distracted that for once she failed to make the obvious riposte.

Frida burst into tears.

Galahad put his arm around the girl. "Whatever is the matter, fair maid?"

Sniff. "Oh Galahad, I've been in love with you forever, and now I've found out that you are gay. Now I'll never get to marry you!" Sob.

"Oh, for goodness sake," said Isabelle, "is that all you can think of right now? Can we have a bit of composure, team?"

She turned to look at Aiofe, but the Irish girl wasn't listening. Her gaze was locked on Perceval and the satyr. One of her hands was caressing the pommel of her sword, and the other was firmly clasped between her legs, fingers working.

Isabelle considered the way that Aiofe's hand was caressing the sword hilt. *So that's why she takes her sword to bed with her*, she thought. *The cunning bitch! I might have to get myself a sword after all.*

Dragging her thoughts back to the present crisis, Isabelle addressed Galahad, who was trying to comfort the weeping Frida. "On your honour, sir knight, I must ask that neither you nor your companion breathe a word of our presence here tonight. If our fathers were to find out, we would be in serious trouble."

"You have my word, dear lady," said Galahad. "And Perceval's as well for he takes his vows as seriously as I do. Neither of us would ever betray a lady's honour. Besides, it is not as if he and I don't have issues of our own. I trust you will be as careful with our secrets as we will be with yours."

"But my stories," wailed Frida, "I'll have to stop writing them. People might guess!"

"Wait," said Galahad. "You're the girl who writes all that Galahad/Perceval slash?"

"Well, most of it," sniffed Frida, drawing herself up. "The better stories, anyway."

Galahad went down on one knee before her. "Then both Perce and I owe you a huge favour, my lady. For it was while laughing together over one of your fine stories that we first discovered our mutual desire. Without you, we might never have come out to each other."

"Really?" asked Frida, brightening visibly.

"Upon my honour, dear lady," said Galahad, extravagantly kissing her hand. "And don't worry about stopping. Your writing is the best cover we could wish for. No one would guess that our relationship was real with those stories doing the rounds of the court."

Frida swooned, and Galahad gathered her up with the

practiced arm of a man who is entirely too used to ladies swooning in front of him.

"Oh, Maeve's titties," said Aiofe, looking a little flushed. "We didn't come here to swoon over kisses on the hand; we came here to get laid."

"Succinctly, if inelegantly, put," said Isabelle.

"Well," said Galahad, "it appears to be down to me to find a solution to this. Perceval is the fittest of Arthur's knights. The satyr will doubtless tire him eventually, at which point I hope to take my turn, but we probably have a few hours yet."

"Do you have any suggestions, Sir knight?" asked Isabelle. "I understand that we might not be entirely to your taste, but we are all three in a state of some distress."

"I might do," said Galahad. "As I understand it, you ladies came here tonight to avail yourselves of some lessons in the arts of love. How about we start with some definitions? Are you, perchance, familiar with the term, *bisexual?*"

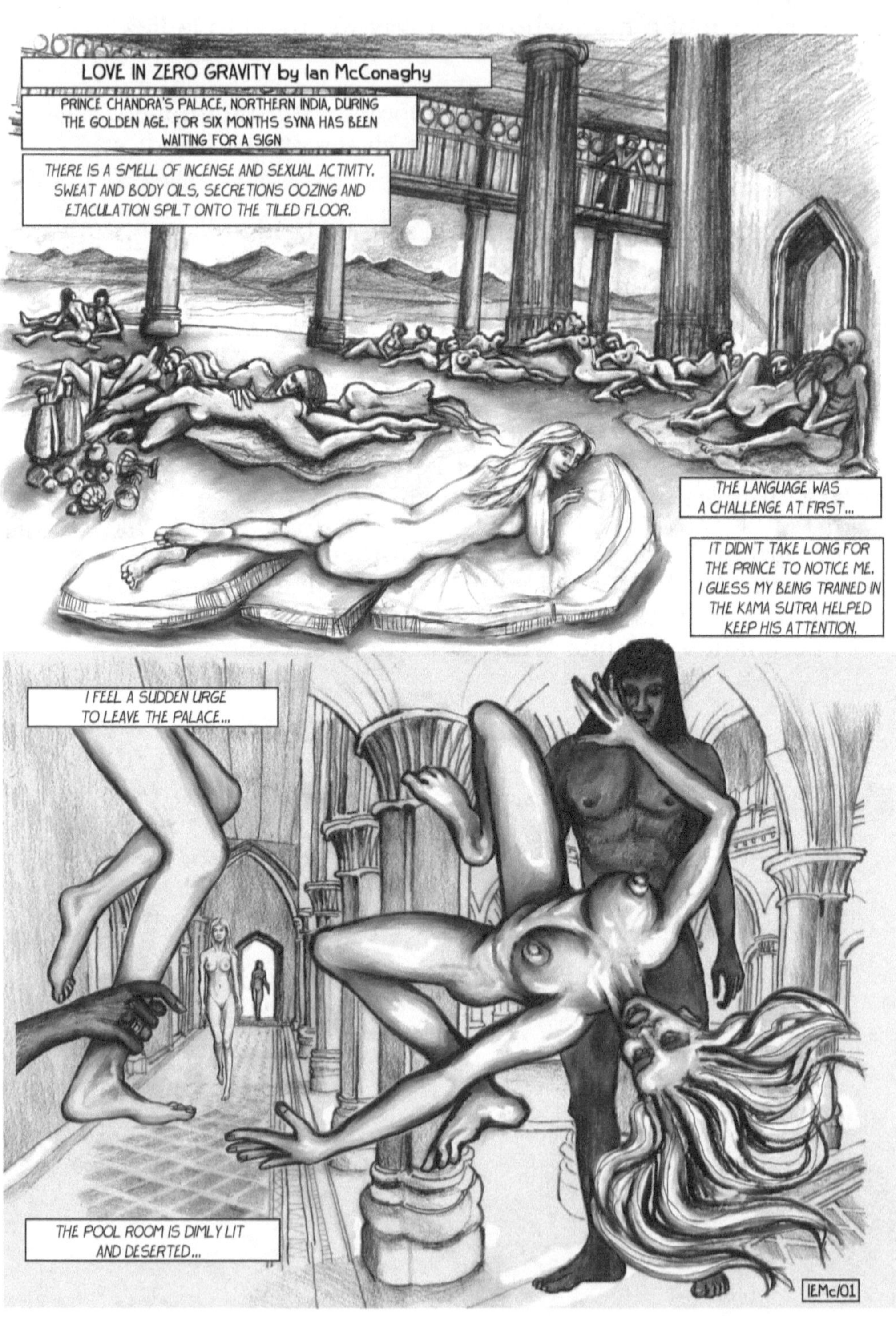

LOVE IN ZERO GRAVITY by Ian McConaghy
PRINCE CHANDRA'S PALACE, NORTHERN INDIA, DURING THE GOLDEN AGE. FOR SIX MONTHS SYNA HAS BEEN WAITING FOR A SIGN
THERE IS A SMELL OF INCENSE AND SEXUAL ACTIVITY. SWEAT AND BODY OILS, SECRETIONS OOZING AND EJACULATION SPILT ONTO THE TILED FLOOR.
THE LANGUAGE WAS A CHALLENGE AT FIRST...
IT DIDN'T TAKE LONG FOR THE PRINCE TO NOTICE ME. I GUESS MY BEING TRAINED IN THE KAMA SUTRA HELPED KEEP HIS ATTENTION.
I FEEL A SUDDEN URGE TO LEAVE THE PALACE...
THE POOL ROOM IS DIMLY LIT AND DESERTED...
IEMc/01

BEAUTIFUL SYNA! I HAVE BEEN WAITING FOR YOU ALL EVENING.
I HAVE RESERVED ONE SPECIAL SPURT OF PLEASURE JUST FOR YOU.
E! YOU HAVE THE BODY OF A WARRIOR.
MAY YOUR SWORD FILL ME TO THE HILT.
MMM!... AH! AH! AH!
RIDE ME ACROSS THE PLAINS OF PASSION UNTIL DAWN BREAKS.
DEEPER, DEEPER - THERE'S STILL ROOM FOR MORE.
IT IS TIME! AHHHHHHH!
WHAT'S HAPPENING? I CAN FEEL IT PLAINLY, A JOLT TO MY BODY. I MUST LEAVE.
WHERE CAN I RENDEZVOUS?
IEMc /02

THE CONTACT TATTOO O
MY ARM REALLY IS THROBBINC
SO YOU ARE TRYING TO LEAVE!
I THINK MY CATS WILL ENJOY SOME SPORT.
WHAT A STINK, AND THAT NOISE.
TIGERS!
RRRAARRR
GRRR RAAR RAAR!
WILL I GET TO THE CLIF

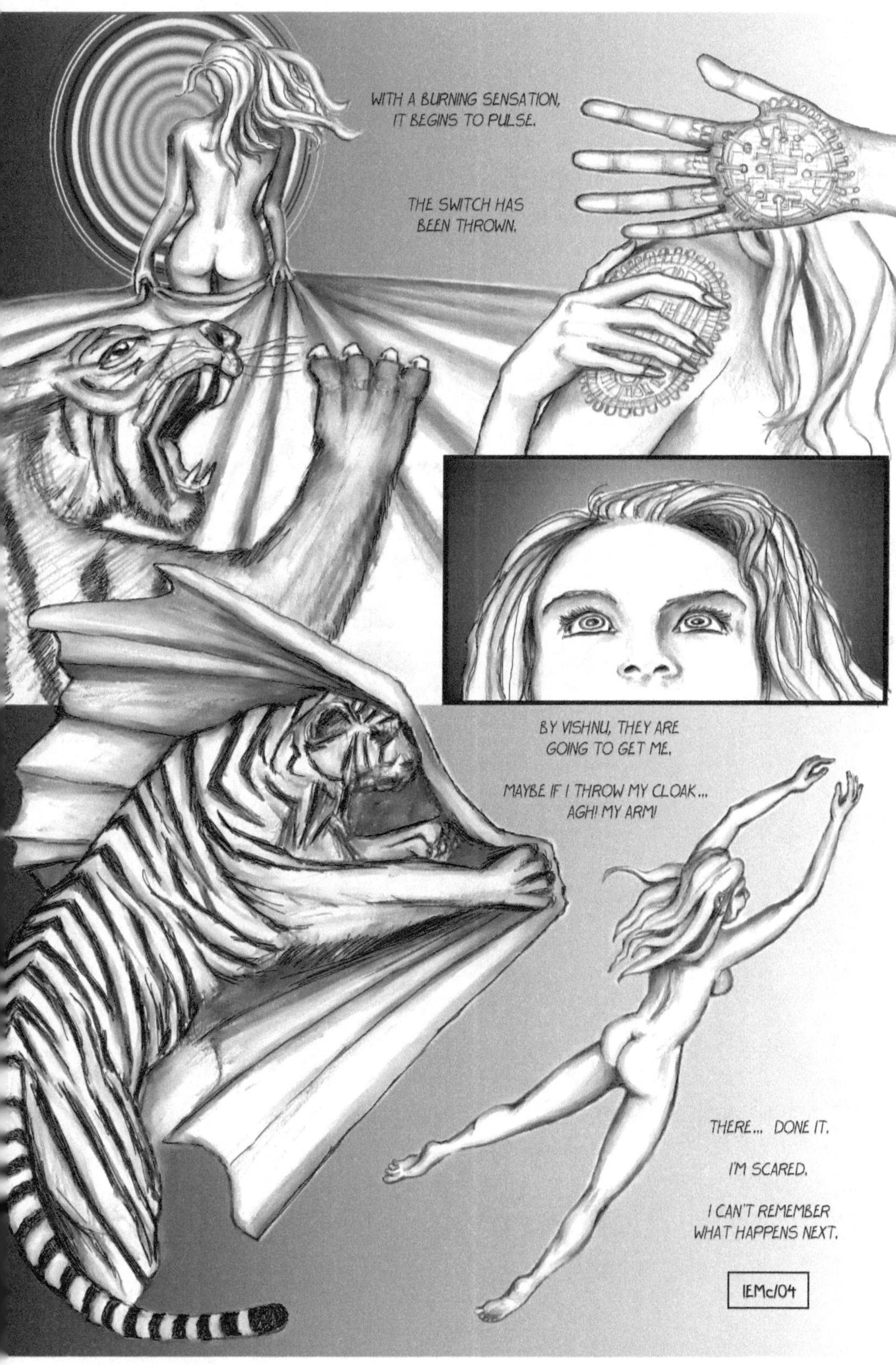

WITH A BURNING SENSATION, IT BEGINS TO PULSE.

THE SWITCH HAS BEEN THROWN.

BY VISHNU, THEY ARE GOING TO GET ME.

MAYBE IF I THROW MY CLOAK... AGH! MY ARM!

THERE... DONE IT.

I'M SCARED.

I CAN'T REMEMBER WHAT HAPPENS NEXT.

IEMc/04

I DIDN'T EXPECT THEM TO COME FOR YOU.
SOMEHOW, THEY MANAGED TO REPAIR...
NEVER MIND, THE CATS MUST REMAIN HUNGRY THIS TIME.
BUT WE'LL MEET AGAIN SWEET SYNA.
I MUST RELAX
OPEN MY MOUTH AND EYES WIDE
LET THE CRAFT TAKE POSSESSION.
IEMc/05

I CAN SEE HER WITHIN
BUT IT IS DISAPPEARING
FROM VIEW... INTERESTING
NEVER MIND -
I'LL GET ANOTHER CHANCE.

TEN MILLENNIA INTO THE FUTURE.
IEMc/07

S THIS? THE EARTH'S EXPLODING!
ARKS! I'M COMING INTO ARK TWO.
ANAGED TO LEAVE EARTH BEFORE
HE NUCLEAR WAR STARTED...
ND THE LONG COLD WINTER...
Y VISHNU, THIS IS HORRIBLE.
I AM DEAF, DUMB, BLIND...
JUST NEED TO GET RID OF
THIS SO THAT I CAN THINK...
YEUGH! FINALLY!
HOW MANY
MORE TESTS?
HI SYNTH, WELCOME BACK!
IT'S BEEN A LONG TIME.
HOW ABOUT MEETING ME IN
THE ZERO-GRAVITY ROOM?
I'M FEELING
A LITTLE SORE RIGHT NOW.
BUT PERHAPS LATER.
OH... IT'S YOU!
IEMc/08

CLO E, IT'S GOOD TO SEE YOU AGAIN.
I'VE REALLY MISSED YOU SYNTH. FIVE YEARS SINCE THE ACCIDENT.
IT WAS LESS TIME FOR ME ON EARTH. WHAT HAPPENED?
SOON AFTER YOU LEFT THE LAUNCH PAD AND SEVERAL VESSELS WERE DESTROYED.
THANK VISHNU THE VESSEL RETURNED!
THE COMMUNICATION SCANNER WAS ALSO DAMAGED. WE LOST TOUCH WITH ARK ONE.
ON ARK ONE THEY MUST BE ABOUT TO EMERGE FROM THEIR HIBERNATION PODS.
IS THERE ANY NEWS FROM EARTH?
STORMS AND 'QUAKES HAVE BEEN MAKING COMMUNICATIONS DIFFICULT.
ARE THERE SURVIVORS?
IEMc

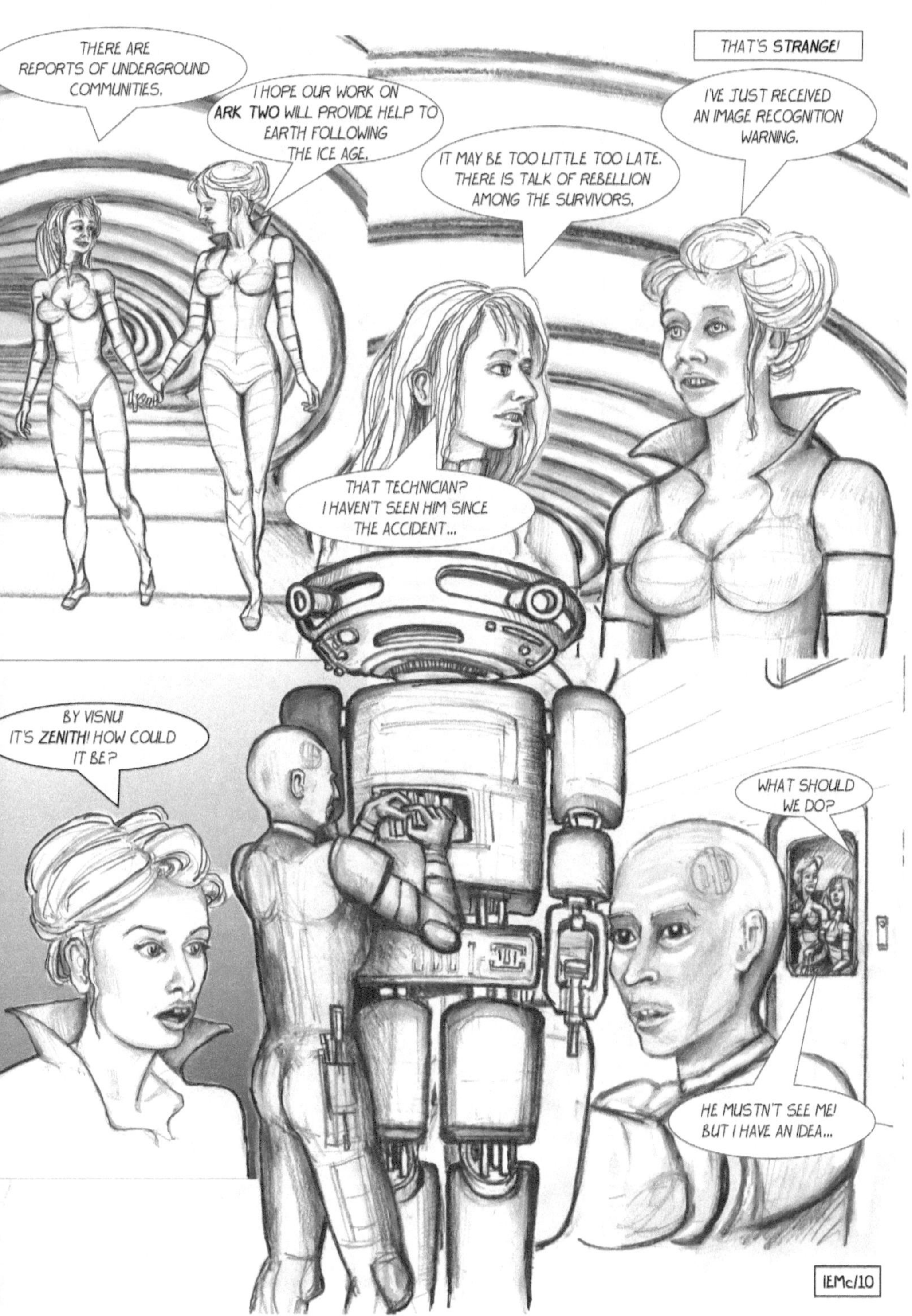

THERE ARE REPORTS OF UNDERGROUND COMMUNITIES.
I HOPE OUR WORK ON ARK TWO WILL PROVIDE HELP TO EARTH FOLLOWING THE ICE AGE.
IT MAY BE TOO LITTLE TOO LATE. THERE IS TALK OF REBELLION AMONG THE SURVIVORS.
THAT'S STRANGE!
I'VE JUST RECEIVED AN IMAGE RECOGNITION WARNING.
THAT TECHNICIAN? I HAVEN'T SEEN HIM SINCE THE ACCIDENT...
BY VISNU! IT'S ZENITH! HOW COULD IT BE?
WHAT SHOULD WE DO?
HE MUSTN'T SEE ME! BUT I HAVE AN IDEA...
IEMc/10

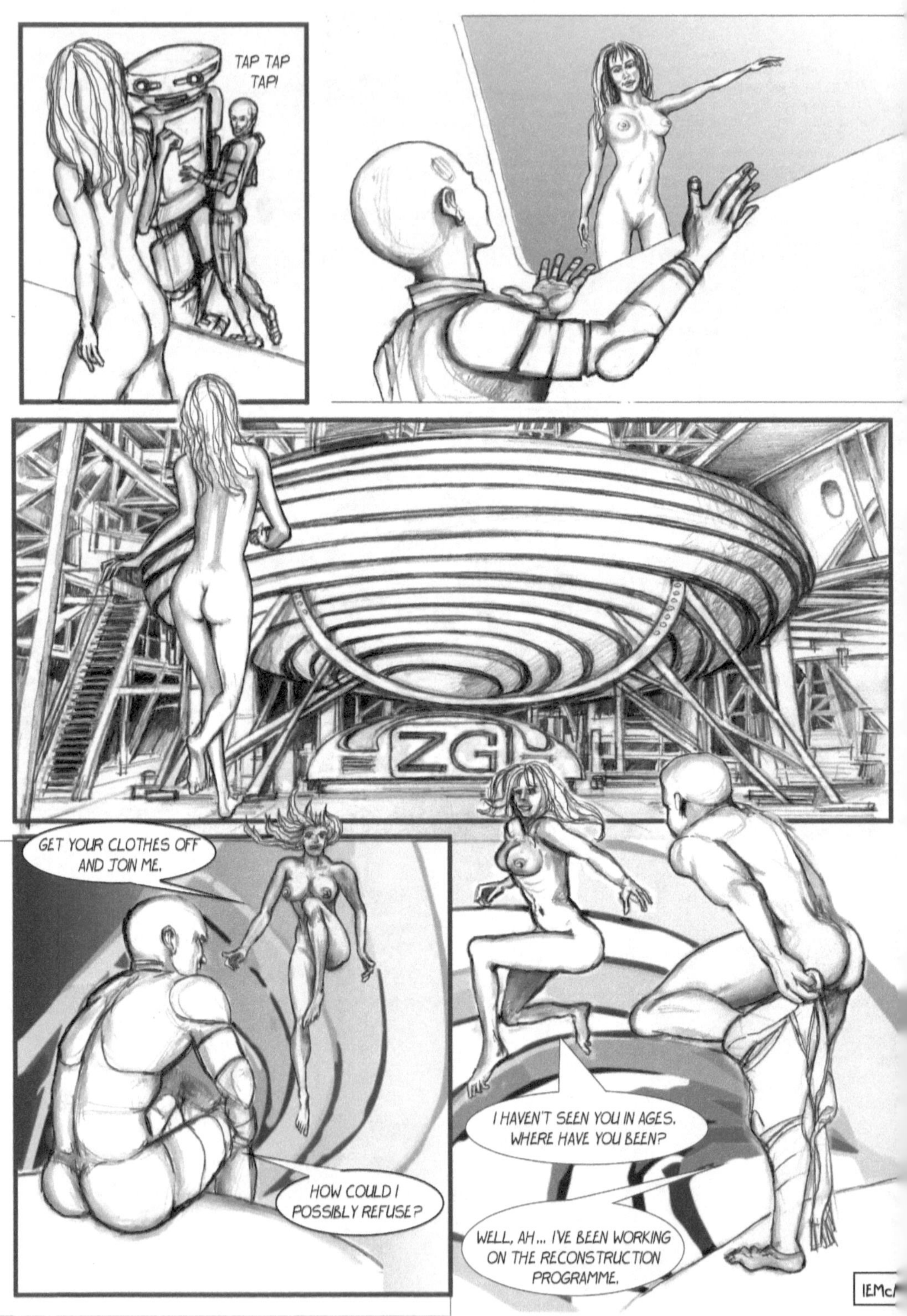

TAP TAP TAP!
GET YOUR CLOTHES OFF AND JOIN ME.
HOW COULD I POSSIBLY REFUSE?
I HAVEN'T SEEN YOU IN AGES. WHERE HAVE YOU BEEN?
WELL, AH... I'VE BEEN WORKING ON THE RECONSTRUCTION PROGRAMME.
ZG

IS THERE ANY NEWS FROM ARK ONE?
NONE BUT WE SHOULDN'T WASTE OUR TIME ON THEM!
WE MUST HELP EARTH.
THE SCANNER IS REPAIRED. WE MUST CONTACT EARTH.
AREN'T ALL COMMUNICATIONS DOWN?
YOU'RE RIGHT. WE MUST FIND SURVIVORS.
BUT NO MORE TALKING...
LET'S MAKE LOVE.
IEMc/12

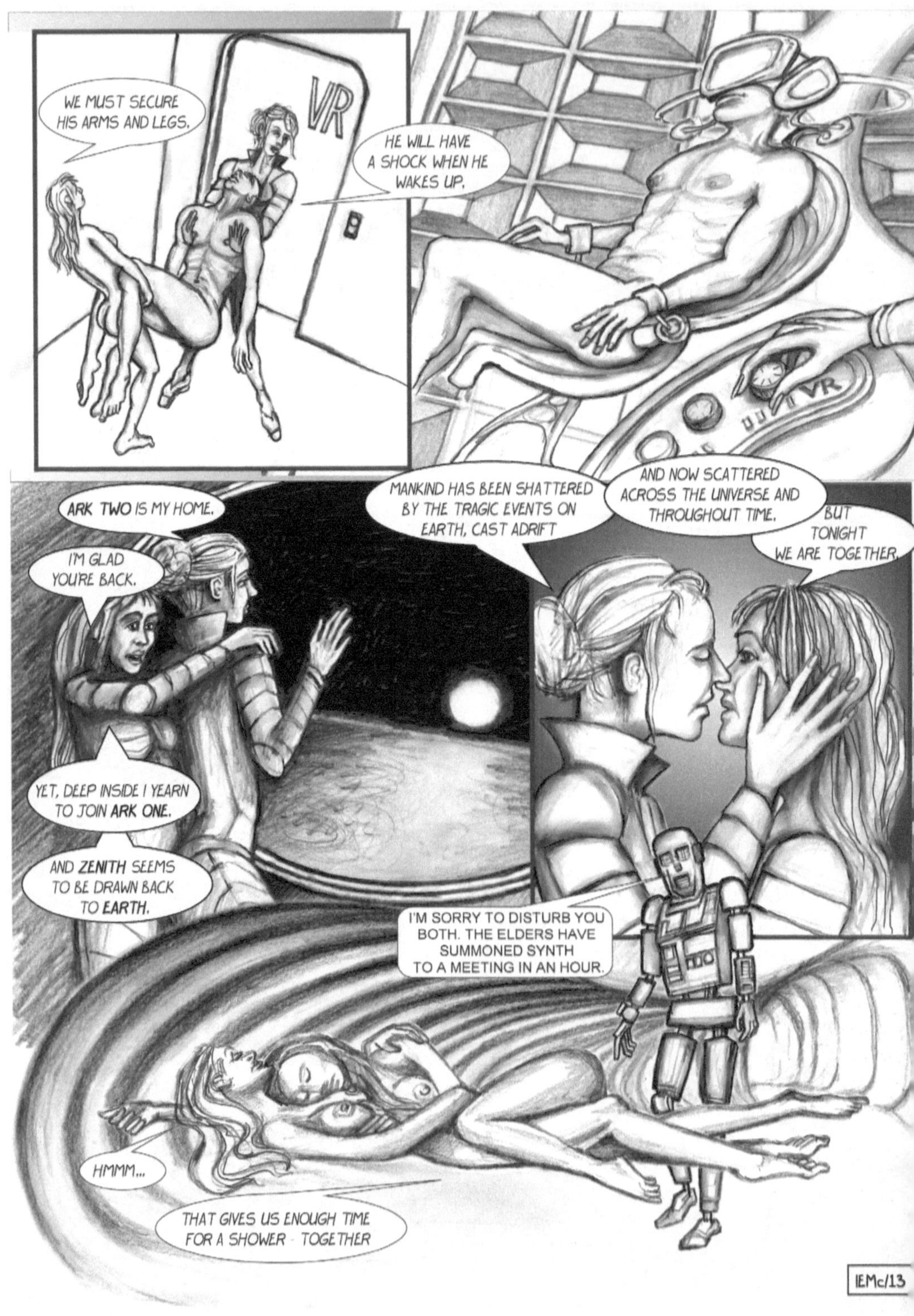

WE MUST SECURE HIS ARMS AND LEGS.
HE WILL HAVE A SHOCK WHEN HE WAKES UP.
VR
ARK TWO IS MY HOME.
I'M GLAD YOU'RE BACK.
YET, DEEP INSIDE I YEARN TO JOIN ARK ONE.
AND ZENITH SEEMS TO BE DRAWN BACK TO EARTH.
MANKIND HAS BEEN SHATTERED BY THE TRAGIC EVENTS ON EARTH, CAST ADRIFT
AND NOW SCATTERED ACROSS THE UNIVERSE AND THROUGHOUT TIME.
BUT TONIGHT WE ARE TOGETHER.
I'M SORRY TO DISTURB YOU BOTH. THE ELDERS HAVE SUMMONED SYNTH TO A MEETING IN AN HOUR.
HMMM...
THAT GIVES US ENOUGH TIME FOR A SHOWER - TOGETHER
IEMc/13

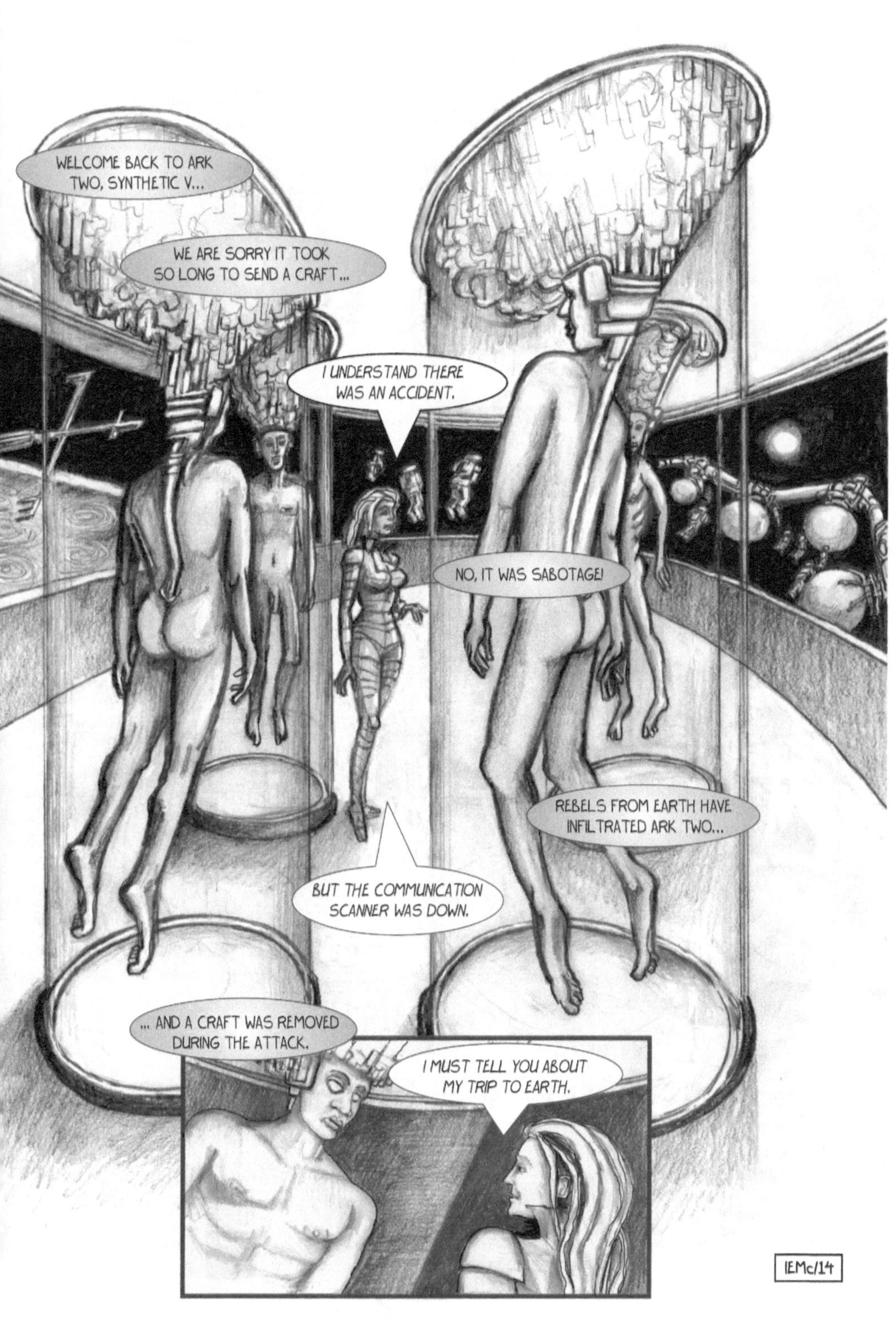

WELCOME BACK TO ARK TWO, SYNTHETIC V...
WE ARE SORRY IT TOOK SO LONG TO SEND A CRAFT...
I UNDERSTAND THERE WAS AN ACCIDENT.
NO, IT WAS SABOTAGE!
BUT THE COMMUNICATION SCANNER WAS DOWN.
REBELS FROM EARTH HAVE INFILTRATED ARK TWO...
... AND A CRAFT WAS REMOVED DURING THE ATTACK.
I MUST TELL YOU ABOUT MY TRIP TO EARTH.
IEMc/14

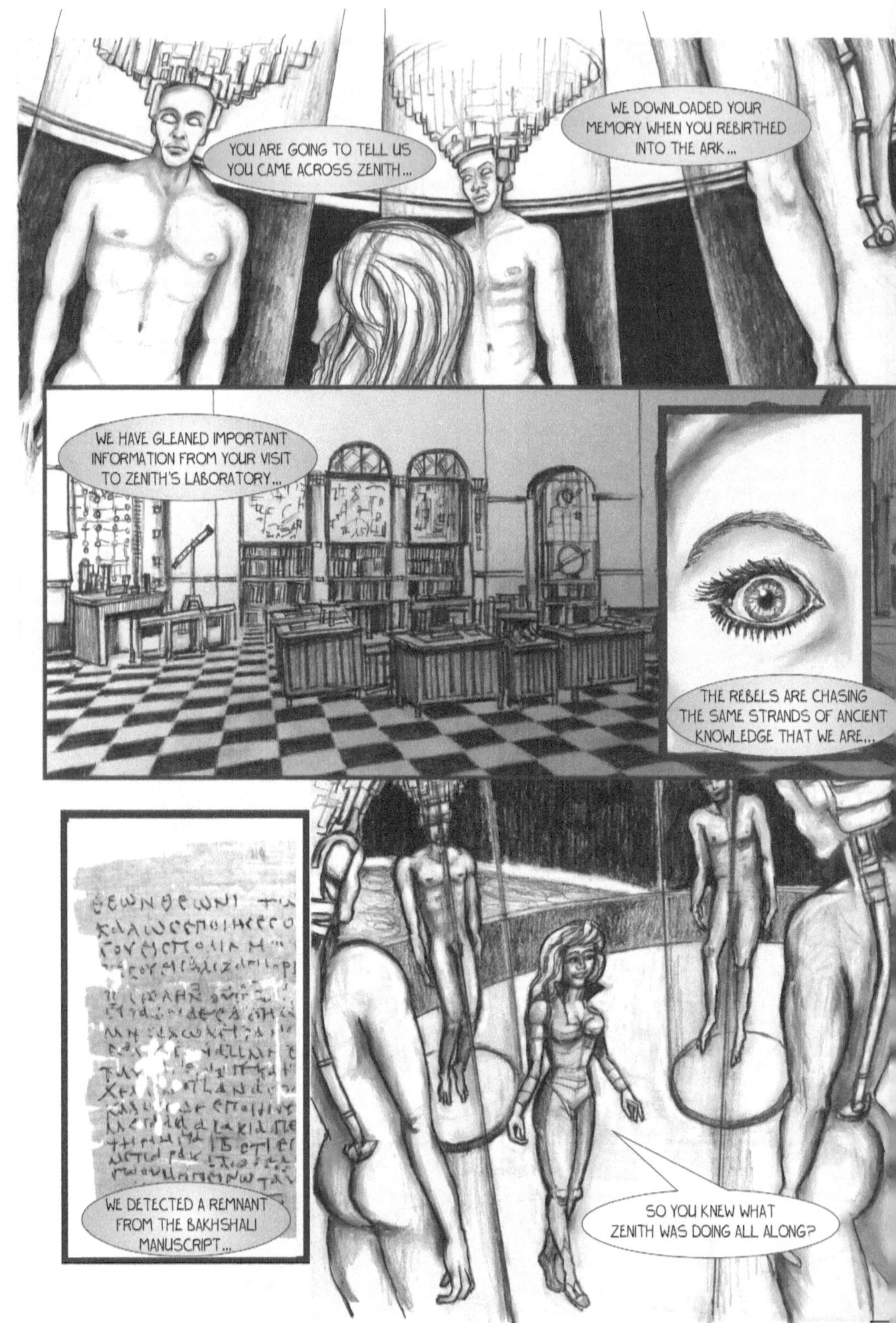

YOU ARE GOING TO TELL US YOU CAME ACROSS ZENITH...
WE DOWNLOADED YOUR MEMORY WHEN YOU REBIRTHED INTO THE ARK...
WE HAVE GLEANED IMPORTANT INFORMATION FROM YOUR VISIT TO ZENITH'S LABORATORY...
THE REBELS ARE CHASING THE SAME STRANDS OF ANCIENT KNOWLEDGE THAT WE ARE...
WE DETECTED A REMNANT FROM THE BAKHSHALI MANUSCRIPT...
SO YOU KNEW WHAT ZENITH WAS DOING ALL ALONG?

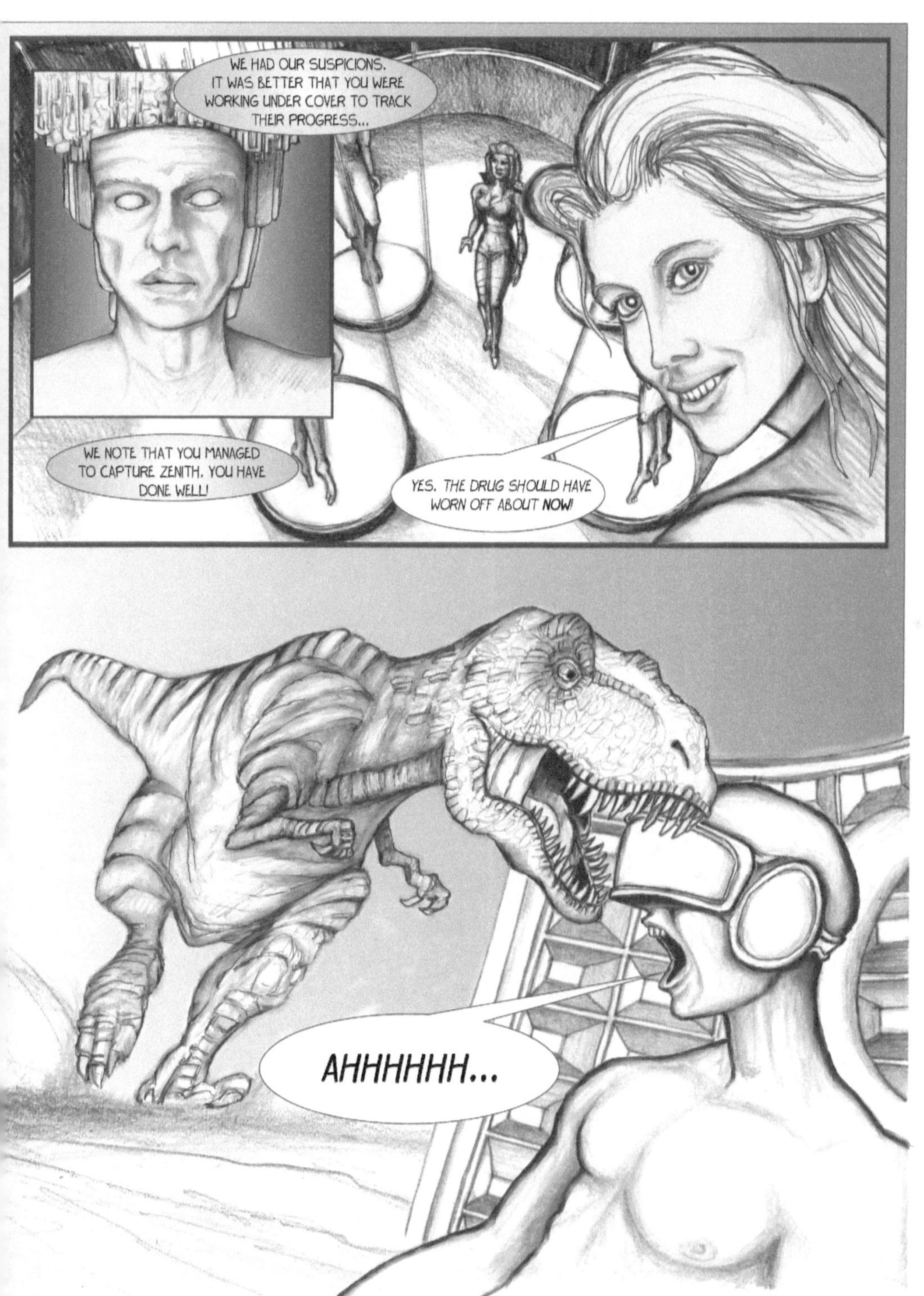
WE HAD OUR SUSPICIONS.
IT WAS BETTER THAT YOU WERE
WORKING UNDER COVER TO TRACK
THEIR PROGRESS...
WE NOTE THAT YOU MANAGED
TO CAPTURE ZENITH. YOU HAVE
DONE WELL!
YES. THE DRUG SHOULD HAVE
WORN OFF ABOUT NOW!
AHHHHHH...
IM/up dated 05/08/2016

Horny Sci-fi

Subject 93-A

By R. J. H.

"This is just sad, Will," James said as he flipped through Will's cable package. "You've got what? Like, five thousand channels? And there's nothing on?"

"There's always something. You're just not looking hard enough."

Jason looked at Will and pressed the remote's button harder. He looked back at the TV.

"Nope, still nothing."

"All right, fine, try—What time is it? Four-ish? Okay, try thirteen twenty-seven."

James punched in the number and was greeted by a man speaking a language that he couldn't even identify and cooking something equally unbeknownst. He tried the number again, only to find that he had done so correctly.

"This?" James asked.

"Yeah, this guy is great. Last week he made something that looked amazing."

James's eyes scrunched.

"I mean, I think it looked amazing. I assume it was supposed to come out the way it did."

"Okay, speaking of 'out,' I think we need to be. Right now. The thing about you paying for every channel on the planet is no longer the saddest thing."

"I don't get every channel on the planet. There's a few islands in Indonesia that have very local broadcasting that's tough to get over here."

"Right. Well, that unfortunate truth aside, we need to have some fun, especially you. Come on, you can't spend every moment on this settee." James got up and straightened himself. He stood in front of Will expectantly, nodding his head towards the front door. Will's shoulders hunched and he sank into the corduroy waves of the cushions.

"I'm not really in the mood."

James huffed and flung himself back down.

"Well, when are you going to be in the mood, Will? It's been almost five months since that harpy pulled her claws out of you."

"I told you not to call Jennifer that."

"I'm gonna call her that until you snap out of this funk you've put yourself in. Now come on. Let's get ready, go out into the world and watch some very nice non-life-ruining ladies take their clothes off for money."

Will hesitated but again shrank further down into the security of the ribbed, brown fabric.

"I don't think I'm ready for that," Will mumbled as he pretended to be engrossed in the foreign dish being prepared.

"I'm not asking you to find somebody to move in with, Will, but you've got to at least try. Can't we just go out and see some boobs? Don't you remember boobs? You used to love boobs."

"I still do," Will said, sounding like he was trying to convince himself more than James.

"No, I don't feel it," James said, folding his arms. "I remember a man who could hold his own. A man who was there, night after night, on a bar stool with his name carved into it."

"We got in trouble for that."

"A man who once did a shot off of both the waitresses and the girl at the door in a single night."

"That was you."

"That's not the point. The point is, you need to be that guy again. Yes, you gave the whole 'relationship' thing a shot and it blew up in your face. But at least you tried. Try again, this time with a woman who won't treat you like an accessory that she's thinking of getting rid of. Doesn't that sound nice?"

Will sat silently for a moment, still watching the chef chop and fry a mysterious meat.

"Yeah," he finally said, "it does."

"Great! Well, there's only one way that's going to happen. A girl isn't just going to crash through the—"

James was cut off by a thunderous boom as the front door of Will's house was obliterated. Half of the wall came with it as bits of wood, dry wall, and other debris flew through the room. James and Will were blown back as the sheer force of the impact rippled through the space. Picture frames shattered in a wave along the wall as it absorbed the tremendous strike, and the men were thrown to the ground. Will's head smacked into the hardwood floor. He sat bolt upright for a split second, long enough to see James crumple into unconsciousness before succumbing himself to the darkness growing around his vision.

***

Will stirred and rolled around on the floor as he melted back into the world. The room faded into view in blurry patches. His head throbbed. James stood in the middle of the room, silently staring at something. Will rolled over onto his hands and pushed himself up.

"What happened?" Will asked, still regaining his awareness. "James?"

110

James didn't respond. Will followed his gaze to the remains of his foyer. Embedded in the floor, right where Will's doormat had been, was a giant metal orb. It looked perfectly round and smooth like a giant chrome cannonball. Will's eyes went wide. His mouth opened but his throat dried up before he could talk. He swallowed hard and looked at James.

"What the hell is that?" Will asked. The shock had yet to pass, filtering the emotion from his voice.

James inched closer to the ball.

"Hey," Will asked, half-heartedly reaching out for him, never taking his eyes off the object, "what are you doing?"

James reached his hand out towards the thing, sitting in the doorway.

"Wait, that thing's probably—"

James's fingers brushed up against it, and he immediately snapped his arm back.

"Really hot."

James approached again. This time, he let his fingers linger on the ball and then his palm. He shook his head.

"No, it's fine. It's kinda cold, actually."

Will touched the ball with the tip of one finger and felt the cold run up to his first knuckle. He dragged his finger along its surface and a string of lights appeared down its side. Will jumped back and stood behind James. The ball started to whir and hum and an outline appeared across its front. The outline sunk into the ball and slid apart to reveal a creature, limp in a seat surrounded by controls.

"James, is that a—"

"I think it might be."

"What do we do? Is it dead? It looks dead."

"Okay, first let's make sure it is then."

James picked up a shard of wood that had been blasted from Will's house and nudged the creature. It didn't move.

"I think it's dead."

"In terms of the government busting down the rest of my house and taking this thing, is it better if it's alive or dead?"

James poked it again. The creature stirred, and the two stumbled backwards and ducked behind the couch. They peeked up and saw the creature moving.

"Okay, she's definitely alive."

"She?"

"Well, she looks like a she."

Will took a second and looked at her more closely. As far as her stature, she didn't look very different from a human. She wore a garment that covered her from her feet all the way up to her neck. Along the way, it hid some very woman-like features. She was bald, and her skull curved down into a tiny wave at its base. Her temples had defined arches, and her head was the only place her pale skin showed with a slight blue tinge like the hottest stars. Her eyes held the same piercing blue. Will realised too late that he could see her eyes and that she could see him. The two ducked behind the sofa.

"She saw me!"

"I know, stay calm."

"Calm!?"

The two stopped arguing as a groan floated over to them. They looked at each other and then up. The girl had her eyes closed in a wince and had her hands over her ribs. At least that's where Will assumed her ribs were.

"I think she's hurt," Will said, edging out.

"Of course she's hurt; she just crashed here from space! It's a miracle we're both still alive."

Will came out from behind the sofa, followed slowly by James.

"Hey," Will called out. Her eyes shot open. Will froze as she stared at him. "A... are you okay?"

The girl breathed out and winced again.

"I'll get some bandages," Will said and walked into the kitchen.

"Uh, Will, I'm not sure we're the people to be doing this."

"She's hurt, James. We should at least try to help her."

"Yeah, sure, but you don't know what you're doing. Not to mention that you have no idea what her body is like. What if you press a spot on her and she drops dead? This is too much. I need some air."

As James tried to get around the wreckage, the girl made a distressed sound and reached out for him. She immediately recoiled and gripped her ribs.

"She doesn't want you to go."

"Why not?"

"I don't know. She's probably scared."

Will slowly approached the girl with his first-aid kit. She eyed him suspiciously as he opened it. He pulled out a roll of bandages. He pointed at her ribs in an attempt to communicate.

"Here?" he asked. She shifted in her seat. Will apprehensively touched just above her hands, but she recoiled. A high-pitched whine escaped her throat. "Sorry! Sorry."

Will unrolled some cloth and placed it on her stomach. He gingerly took her hand and placed it on top of the strip. Before he could wrap any around her, she picked the cloth off her. She pressed a button on a panel on the inside of her wrist. It made the finger she used glow red. She slid the finger across herself, just under her breasts. It left a trail as it went. She pressed down and the trail shot around her back and connected into a loop. She did the same just below her navel. Her suit rippled and melted away between the two loops, leaving her exposed midriff framed around two perfectly clean cuts. She took the cloth from Will and pressed it against her stomach. He wrapped the bandage around enough times to cover her. She squirmed as the tight bandages gripped her sleek form. When he was done, the girl moved around a little and seemed to be in less distress than before. A tiny smile split her steel-grey lips. She pushed herself up out of her seat and walked over to the sofa. She sat down.

"What are we gonna do with her?" James asked, sitting down on the opposite end of the sofa.

"What do you mean?"

"Well, I think she might be stuck here for a while. I don't know how much punishment that ship can take, but after that landing, I think she might need a new way home."

"I didn't think of that. I guess she'll have to stay here for now."

"Stay here? You can't even stay here. Your front wall is missing!"

Will didn't respond. He paced back and forth in front of them. James and the girl sat on the sofa as if they knew each other.

"Whatever," Will finally said. "Either way, we'll take care of her. For now, at least."

James shrugged.

"Looks like you're staying with us," James said to the girl. She cocked her head to the side. James looked at Will, wondering what to do next. When he looked back, the girl was sitting right next to him. She smiled and put her hand on his leg.

"Uh, Will? What's she doing?"

Will just stared as the girl ran her hand up James's leg and settled on his crotch.

"Will?"

The girl started to rub James's cock through his pants. Her smile widened, and her eyes narrowed.

"Does she know what she's doing?" James asked, his voice wavering.

"I'm pretty sure she knows what's going on," Will said. He sat down on the opposite end of the sofa and watched as the girl touched her wrist and then, with a quick flick of her other, drew a red circle in James's lap. His pants disintegrated and his quickly hardening cock sprang forward.

"Yeah, she looks like she's well aware," Will mumbled. "Seems like she's feeling a lot better, too."

"Tell me about it," James said as the girl gently stroked his shaft.

The girl leaned forward, still smiling. James jumped a little as she moved, still unsure if he should be letting his guard down. She pulled her hand down to the base of his cock as a long, thin, flat tongue slid out from her pursed lips. It wrapped twice around James's shaft and started to contract and separate along him while the end flickered against his head. James moaned and closed his eyes as the alien's tongue touched every inch of him at once. She slowly opened her mouth as the end of her tongue switched to licking the underside.

"Will, this is fucking amazing."

"Uh, dude?"

James opened his eyes and looked at Will before noticing the dagger-like teeth, set in three rows, mere inches from his groin. James jumped back but found himself caught in the corner of the sofa. The alien's tongue sped up. He slumped back, surrendering to the otherworldly sensation. Still he stared at her mouth as it came closer and closer to him. James tensed, but then watched as the teeth retracted up into the girl's gum line before her mouth engulfed him fully. James gasped and threw his head back as the alien's soft tongue and gums worked his engorged cock. She bobbed her head up and down slowly, sending James deeper into her mouth with each go. Finally, she buried her face into James's groin and sent him into her throat.

Without leaving, she turned her head around and looked at Will with seductive eyes. James bit his lip and bucked his hips a few times, making the most of his position. The alien didn't waver, easily accommodating James's cock with her throat as she stared at Will. Her eyes traced down Will as his gaze danced back and forth between her lips wrapped around his friend and the beautiful round ass staring him in the face. She smiled as best she could with a mouth full of James when she saw the growing mass under Will's pants. She twisted her head to the side before bobbing it again. James moaned and slumped, arching his back and doing everything he could to get his cock further inside the girl's throat. He put his hands on the back of her head and guided it down. She put her hand on James's ass and pulled him into her for one final dive before sucking on him as she pulled up and out. James's cock left her mouth with a pop and was eagerly consumed again, right down to his pelvis. The long strokes continued. James ran his hands over his face.

Much to James's dismay, the girl slowed and once again looked back at Will. She saw tightness in his pants. She saw the deep, heavy breaths he was making. She saw the hungry look in his eyes. She pressed a button on her wrist and drew a generous circle from the small of her back to just below her ass. The fiery red circle dissolved the suit within, exposing her beautiful body to the open air. Will groaned, reached into his pants, and rubbed himself. She slowly wiggled her hips at him and went back to sucking on James.

"I don't know about this, James."

"Your loss, man. That's a better invitation than I've ever gotten from anyone."

The girl steadied herself with one hand and let the other roam down her stomach and into the now-exposed patch of skin. Her fingers brushed along the lips of her very human-like vagina and spread them apart for Will to marvel at. As two fingers held her apart, a third rubbed her clitoris and then sunk into her. She pulled it out, wet with need, and rubbed it back across her clit, smoother and faster than before. She moaned as she worked herself, and James lurched forward as it resonated along his shaft.

"Oh, God, keep doing that."

Will watched as the alien's fingers darted in and out of herself, stopping only to give her clit a moment of attention. She glistened as her pleasure mounted. Sweat began to form around Will's forehead as he stroked his cock to the show in front of him. He took off his pants and finally let himself be free. He stroked himself harder and faster as the two came closer to orgasm. Will couldn't take any more. He stood up, one foot on the floor and the other on the sofa as he grabbed the girl's hips in both hands. He pulled her towards him and buried himself inside of her beautiful wet pussy. She squealed and gripped the couch as Will began driving into her, but she didn't draw away from James's lap.

Will pounded his cock into the alien as she sucked James deep into her throat. For a moment, he thrust as hard and as fast as he could, expending the pressure that had built up in his body watching the sexy blue goddess pleasure his friend and herself. When it had passed, he slowed and began to enjoy the feeling of her on him. The texture of her inside glided along his entire length, sending a glorious sensation into his core. Will bit his lip and pushed further in. He wanted to feel every little bit of pleasure that could possibly be felt from this celestial gift. Will squeezed the girl's ass with both hands and continued to push into her. She in turn squeezed back. Her pussy gripped Will and massaged him as he moved inside of her.

"I could die right here and I wouldn't care," Will said as more sensation climbed his cock up into his body. The girl let out a little titter and dove further onto James while simultaneously pushing Will further into herself. Will, lost in pleasure, had a brief moment of lucidity.

"Did she just understand me?" Will asked, still thrusting despite his trepidation.

"Yeah, I'm pretty sure she has a translator or something," James said, somewhat delirious himself.

"How could you possibly know that?"

"I don't, but every time we talk, that thing on her wrist chirps out some weird noises."

Sure enough, as James finished speaking, a strange, barely audible string of sounds played from her wrist. The girl's eyes narrowed, and she manipulated her mouth. James made a noise that Will had never heard before and ran his hands over the girl's head. Likewise, Will felt her clamp down just right and sent a wave of pleasure through his cock. A universal language transcending the English phrase, "Shut up and enjoy this," if there ever was one. Will didn't need the reminder. He picked up the pace and felt the familiar sensation of a building orgasm inside of him.

"James, I don't think I'm gonna last much longer."

"Yeah, I'm almost there, too."

Will's hips started to fail him as the sensations mounted. He pulled and pushed the alien girl along the length of his cock as his body rested. She pushed back, burying Will inside of her and squirming her ass into his pelvis. Will groaned and resumed his normal pace, thrusting deep into the insatiable girl. She grew tighter around him as he pounded into her. She closed her eyes and drew her brows together as she grew closer to the end as well. The extra tightness around him only spurned Will on to get in as much as he could. He opened his eyes for a moment and really took in what he was doing. He saw the beautiful curved shape of the alien girl he was fucking and almost lost it right there. He saw the look on James's face as her tongue and throat worked their magic on him. Then he saw the remaining walls flicker.

Will's eyes went wide. Around him, the entire room went fuzzy, like a TV not tuned properly. It flickered a few more times and then disappeared completely. Will's thrusting slowed and then finally stopped as he saw where he really was, standing in a large dome with his cock engulfed by a beautiful alien girl, while being watched by several others just like her. James, Will, and the girl all froze. One of the aliens furiously pounded at a keyboard while another shouted at him. Another standing next to them seemed only to be taking notes. The girl looked back at Will. Her body twitched, and Will closed his eyes as he felt the shock. She smiled and pushed back, sending Will's cock as deep into her as it would go. He moaned and grabbed her hips. Will and James looked at each other for a second before giving up and continuing the act.

Will felt his cock swell as he pounded into the alien girl. She slid across him as she bounced back and forth between the two, fucking Will on one end and swallowing James on the other. Will felt the urge rising in him as he thrusted and knew he was on the brink. He slowed and savoured the feeling of her one last time before what was next. Beside him, James's pace quickened and his breath caught as he unloaded a stream of cum into her mouth. She jolted in surprise and sank down onto Will. The sensation was enough to send him over the edge. He grabbed her hips and gave the final blissful thrusts as he came hard into her beautiful wet pussy. The two slowed and slumped over, knackered, but they barely had enough time to recover before the other aliens were in the room. The aliens separated them from the girl and collected the cum from her in test beakers. They threw Will's pants at him just in time before he was shuffled onto a teleporter and shot into space. The last thing Will saw before the dazzling light of the sun covered his vision was the girl, giving him a smile and a kiss from across the room.

They materialized across the road from Will's house. The front was still destroyed. Neighbours and cops had since surrounded it. Will put his pants on before anyone noticed.

"Well, at least they didn't probe us," James said as if the experience had been casual. Will looked at him and silently shook his head. "So, you gonna go deal with that?"

Will looked across the street. He sighed and looked off into the sky.

"Nah, let's go do something."

Mind over Matter

By Fifi Nicks

He'd dreamt of her often; the glances he caught of her around the ship were always at a distance, yet now she was in his cabin, an arm's reach away. The first officer rubbed his eyes, but as they refocused, she was still there, draped in a large cream gown from his en-suite, anticipating his next move. He pinched her mocha leg peeping out – it felt real. She responded with a giggle. Though he'd only ever heard her sing before, it seemed to suit her. Aye, perched on the bed in front of him was his dream girl. He didn't need to think how or why, she just was. Melody, a name befitting of a woman who sang on spaceliners, beckoned for him to come join her. Sancus closed his gaping mouth and, as he moved from the chair, swiped the glass at the bedside and downed the cool liquid.

"Oh sorry, did you… ?" he said, sitting beside her.

Shaking her head, she took the glass from his hand and placed it back down, the bathrobe opening as she bent. He flushed as he followed the under-curve of her breast then felt his temperature rise when she caught him looking. Smirking, Melody shrugged off one shoulder of her gown, then the other, letting it glide down her back. The singer was much younger than his wife but a developed woman nevertheless. He tried to shake the latter from his mind, physically.

"What's up?" she said.

"Nothing."

"Don't you like what you see?"

"Quite the opposite."

She smiled, then with a smooth voice said, "I know. I've seen the way you stare at me."

Sancus flinched. He thought his yearnings were discreet. Guilt flooded his mind.

Melody leant forward and began undoing his tie. "Surely you're not shy, Mister First Officer," she said, using it to draw him close then breathed into his ear, "Sir?"

Whatever thoughts consuming Sancus were sucked through the porthole into space that instant.

"No!" He gripped her wrists and coughed. She grinned. "It's just now I've the chance to look at you fully, I'm going to take all of you in."

Placing her away from him, he let his eyes run free. They stroked down her soft neck and swooped up the gentle dips between her shoulders, over her full, brown breasts and around her darker nipples. They traced the wave that narrowed at her waist and back out to her hips. Looking up, he saw flashing out from under jet-black ringleted hair a pair of eyes that bore a resemblance to the rice fields back on Earth. Stark contrasts had always attracted Sancus; his redhead wife's eyes were Neptune-blue. They flickered into view for an instant and he found himself shaking his head again.

"Touch me," Melody said, pulling his hand down and uncrossing her legs. Her urgency was surprising, but Sancus wouldn't spoil it complaining. He dipped under the gown and slipped over her smooth, hairless skin until he felt her wetness. If that didn't indicate her readiness for him, the fact she all but ripped him out of his shirt before pouncing on his belt did. He couldn't believe what was happening; he'd relegated an evening with his dream girl to pure fantasy. Lying back, he shuddered as she pulled his dick into her mouth. She moved so fast he thought he'd explode there and then. As if reading his thoughts, she pulled away with a resonant pop and reached over to the glass.

"Dim," Sancus said, and the cabin lights followed his command. He heard crunching, and a frigid tongue running over his nipple confirmed the sound. He pulled her up to kiss her large violet lips. As he ran the backs of his nails down her side, she passed the remaining ice over. He used it to nibble her earlobe and run it down her neck as he dug his fingers into her ass cheeks. She moaned and rubbed herself against him, her moistened lips separating around his shaft. Reaching under, she held the tip at her opening then arched back upright.

"Now, I'm going to take all of you in," she said, then released, sliding herself down onto it. He grabbed her by the midriff, thrusting that final inch then lifted her in gentle bobbing motions until the whole of his dick was wet.

"Fuck me, Sanky."

The silhouette above him wavered and he froze.

"What now?"

"Only Cytherea calls me Sanky."

"Well your wife ain't here, honey, your dream girl is." She rose and sank back down. "I'm all yours, now fuck me!"

"No."

He rolled her over and saw Melody again in the lowlight, but the image of the singer pixelated as he reached behind his ear. By the time he'd pulled out the chip, she was replaced in full by Cytherea, frowning.

"What happened?" his wife said.

"I can't do it," he said.

"But... I thought you wanted her?"

"Not like this."

"Sanky." She sat up and sighed. "You know I can't share you with anyone."

"Yet you're happy to let me use one of these damned things?" He tossed the Cheatchip towards the bin.

"You agreed to it."

"Your idea, remember."

"You're the one who wants to sleep with other people!"

"But I never wanted to cheat! I want to open our marriage, in an honest way, the chip feels wrong."

Cytherea turned away from him and lay down, staring out the porthole. "In all those galaxies, I want only you."

"Hey." Sancus followed, hugging her from behind, "I want you too... as you, not acting as someone else."

Back came a broken voice, "But you also want others."

"That doesn't change how I feel about you." He squeezed her hand. "You know that right?"

She rolled to face him, nodding.

"I need to feel it too," she said. Her eyes were even brighter behind tears.

His mouth opened to respond, but she closed it with a kiss.

"Make love to me, Sanky."

Love At Solar System's End

By Kevin L. Jones

Life was hard and lonely on the refuelling platform that orbited Jupiter, but that was the way that Keith Sterling liked it. Occasionally he would miss the comforts of the fair sex, but it was a small price to pay to be away from the foul, cramped living conditions back on Mother Earth. Here in space everything was clean, still, and best of all quiet. Keith loved the silence and isolation of deep space. It made his skin crawl when he thought back on his childhood, which was spent crammed into the one-bedroom government apartment assigned to his parents and four brothers and sisters. No, he did not care if he ever saw his home planet again. Here on the refuelling platform he was free. He could do as he pleased, and best of all, he was almost always alone.

Although the orbiting facility was mammoth, roughly the size of Rhode Island, he was its only crew member, and even he was superfluous. The station was completely automated. Luckily for him, the company that employed him did not feel comfortable having such a fantastically expensive piece of equipment floating around in space without some human oversight. He would only come into contact with another human being about once a month when the captain of the supply vessel or of a ship full of emigrants headed to the outer colonies would stay with him for about twelve hours while their craft was refuelled. Fortunately, he would only have to tolerate one person invading his privacy at a time; usually the rest of the visiting ship's complement would be in cryosleep. Happily for Keith, there were no ships scheduled for refuelling any time soon, and he had the whole station to himself.

For some the isolation would have been too much, but not Keith. He had hobbies to occupy his time. When he wasn't busy running the seemingly endless series of maintenance checks on the station, he read discs that contained almost every book ever written. He had a never ending supply of recorded movies and television shows, and when he got lonely, there was a wide variety of pornographic materials that he never seemed to tire of watching. Lately his viewing of the adult films was taking up more and more of his time. So much so that it was actually interfering with his work. One model in particular had captured his imagination, a voluptuous, blonde goddess who went by the name of Pattie Melt.

While totally engrossed in one of Pattie's X-rated performances, it took Keith several minutes to notice that sirens were shrieking all around him. Every proximity alarm within the station screamed. Keith ran to the bridge, checked the scopes, and saw that a meteor or piece of space debris was on a collision course with the platform. Keith's eyes stayed riveted to the flashing screens before him. It was too late for anything to be done. Whatever the unknown object was it was going to strike the station within seconds. As he looked at the scopes in horror, time seemed to stand still. Then something that defied logic occurred. Just before the hurtling object was about to strike and blow the station to bits, it seemed to vanish completely from the universe.

The blaring proximity alarms ceased, and he stood trembling before the consoles, wondering what had just happened and how he was still alive. When he had composed himself sufficiently, he began the long series of system checks and found that everything seemed to be as it should. After hours of running redundant tests he felt completely and utterly spent. He stumbled to his quarters and collapsed in his bunk. As he lay there semi-conscious, he got the feeling that he was not alone. A strange, shadowy blue form stirred in the dark corners of his room. Keith tried to focus on the spectral figure, but every time he did this it seemed to fade away.

After a few minutes, he convinced himself that his eyes had been playing tricks on him, and he soon drifted into a fitful slumber. That night he dreamed of Pattie Melt. This was not an uncommon occurrence. He dreamt of her quite often but never as vividly as this. He could feel the warmth of her soft flesh pressed against his own. As he placed one of her ample breasts in his mouth, he could feel her nipple grow erect. Keith was rudely awakened by yet another orchestra of howling alarms, and he was shocked to see that Pattie Melt still straddled his prone form. Her impossible presence here did not disturb him. In fact, it seemed somehow right to him, righter than anything had ever felt in his entire life. As he frantically thrust himself in and out of the adult actress who passed away years before he had been born, he did not care that the station's power and fuel were being siphoned off. As each system sputtered and failed, Keith did not mind as long as she was with him. Even as the life support systems shut down and the station went dark, Keith smiled happily. He continued to make love to the woman of his dreams. He had finally found the happiness that had always eluded him here at the end of the solar system.

The Way You Make Me Feel

By John Seavey

Tamsin really didn't know what she was going to do when Chandra answered the door. She'd been steeling herself for this all day, obsessively checking and double-checking the psionic shield and wishing that she could do more than just diagnostics – all it did when she wore it was give her a thundering headache. She wouldn't really know if it worked until she ran into an active psi. And she couldn't go find one without admitting what they'd done.

She'd run all sorts of different scenarios in her head as she went through the day's classes, planning for contingencies and rehearsing speeches and imagining that moment when Chandra first saw her, over and over and over again. She'd imagined guilt, fear, defiance, anger, and she'd imagined her reactions to each one. She'd thought about this moment so many times that she didn't know how she'd handle it when it happened.

So when the door slid open, it was as much of a surprise to Tamsin as to Chandra when Tamsin punched her in the face.

Chandra's head snapped back with a satisfying smack, and she staggered backwards through the open doorway with an expression of confusion and pain on her face. "Wha?" she slurred out. Her left eye was already beginning to swell up. She put up her hands defensively, but Tamsin had taken three years of unarmed combat training with Chandra. She knew she could take Chandra. She stepped through the door and let it slide shut behind her.

Behind Chandra, Tamsin could see Gilly kneeling on the floor, nude, with her eyes closed. She had her hands tied behind her back and her ankles tied together, and she was letting out a slow, whimpering moan as she gently shuddered in obvious pleasure. Even if it hadn't been clear from her voice, her indigo nipples stood up like pencil erasers on her lavender breasts. She wore a set of earbuds, and between that and the impressive sex toy between her legs, she was so utterly lost in her own sensations that she was oblivious even to the dust-up going on right in front of her. That made Tamsin really want to give Chandra a matching shiner on her other eye, but she controlled herself. Barely.

Instead, she snarled out, "Did you really think we wouldn't find out what you did to her, you bitch?" Tamsin figured she could always hit her again if she didn't like the answer. And she was pretty sure she wasn't going to like the answer very much.

Chandra brought a hand up to her cheek and touched it gingerly. She winced, then shook her head just a little to clear it. "I... I don't understand, Tam," she said, her voice still a little muzzy. "Last week, you said you wouldn't tell anyone. You said that you didn't want us to get expelled—"

"Last week," Tamsin growled, "I didn't know what you were." She felt a hot rush of righteous anger flush through her body at the look of fear on Chandra's face. "Yeah, that's right. I was a little suspicious after we talked, so I got Karrick to hack into the student databases, have a little look at your personnel file."

Chandra flushed red in all of the places that weren't already swollen with blood. "That is personal and private information!" she hissed. "You had absolutely no right to—"

"Oh, don't you dare start an ethics debate with me!" Tamsin spat out the words as the anger, and the throbbing in her skull that told her the psi-blocker was still working combined to leave her teetering on the edge of violence. "Not with Gilly right there!" Gilly started to open her eyes now, the loud mention of her name sinking in through whatever was playing on the earbuds. Her gaze looked unfocused and glassy, like someone waking from a pleasant dream. "Karrick did what he had to do for a friend. So did I."

Chandra shook her head slowly. "I know what you're thinking, Tam, but—"

"No, you don't," Tamsin replied smugly. She tapped the metal band around her head. "Not while I'm wearing this. I read your file, remember? 'Grade One Telepath.' I took precautions before I came to visit you. So don't even try anything."

Chandra reached up to rub her head, but stopped as she touched the tender bruises blossoming over her left eye. "Tam... I wish I could have told you, but... you've seen how much bias there is against me just for being from the Europa Colonies. Half the people here think I'm some sort of Secessionist sleeper agent. You're one of the only people who accepted me for who I was. I didn't want to wreck it by telling you I was also a psi."

"Oh, but you're perfectly willing to wreck Gilly, huh?" Tamsin took another step forward, feeling grim satisfaction in the way that Chandra took a step back. "Perfectly willing to screw up her academic career, wreck her chances for a starship posting, get her expelled for fraternizing with a fellow student, and leave her some sort of brainwashed sex toy just so that you can get your kicks!" She moved closer. Chandra's back hit the wall.

Behind Tamsin, Gilly muttered out, "No, wait... " but Tamsin didn't listen. Gilly wouldn't have anything useful to say until Chandra fixed what she'd done to her. And when she did, Tamsin was going to hold Chandra down while Gilly really went to work on the bitch.

"Brainwashed... " Chandra looked at her in utter astonishment. And then, unbelievably, she started laughing. "Oh, Veda," she gasped out between peals of helpless laughter. "Oh, Veda, you thought that I... that I... " Then she lost it again, giggling hysterically as she sank down along the wall.

"Stop it!" Tamsin yelled, her face red with fury. She

wanted so bad to kick Chandra in the ribs, but she couldn't bring herself to do it. "None of this is fucking funny!" It was a good thing that the walls of the dorms were sound-proofed. Right now, if a proctor walked in on this, they'd probably all three get booted from the Academy. Two naked girls, a third girl fighting with one of them, kinky bondage games going on – it would definitely not look good on their academic record, to say the least.

Which was half of why Tamsin was so pissed at Chandra. She and Gilly had been into each other for a while now, and nobody really cared – the 'no fraternizing' rule was on the books, but the instructors never really enforced it unless it got in the way of classwork. But lately, Gilly had been getting more daring. Nothing that would get her expelled, yet, but things that her friends had started to notice. Coming to classes still smelling of sex, slipping off to make out during free periods... Tamsin had actually noticed her fingering herself below her desk during Astronavigation 301. Sooner or later, someone was bound to crack down on them.

Tamsin had tried to tell them that the first time she'd walked in on them like this, a week ago. (After blushing furiously, spinning around, and trying desperately to pretend she hadn't seen two of her closest friends buck naked and fucking each other.) They'd both waved it off, but Tamsin hadn't liked the way Gilly had been so unconcerned about it. She'd seemed so studious when she'd first come to the Academy. Admittedly, Sirians had that reputation, but it still felt out of character to Tamsin. That was when she'd gone to Karrick, asked him to use that way he had with computers to find out a little bit more about Chandra Sayani. And what he'd found...

Tamsin couldn't help herself anymore. She grabbed Chandra by the shoulders and shook her furiously. "Stop it!" she shouted. "You get a hold of yourself, and you fix what you've done to Gilly, and you do it now!" But Chandra didn't stop laughing. Tamsin suspected the other girl really was hysterical now, but she couldn't stop herself from shaking

Chandra any more than the other girl could get rid of the giggles.

It might have gotten bad, then, if not for Gilly. She must have managed to get to her feet somehow, because she hopped her way over to Tamsin and flung her body against Tamsin's back in an attempt to somehow rescue her girlfriend. It didn't exactly work – she couldn't put much momentum into it, and she lost her balance and fell down while barely even nudging the other girl. But it was enough to snap Tamsin out of her rage, just a little. She let go of Chandra and began to help Gilly back up to a sitting position.

Chandra finally began to calm down, as well. "I'm sorry," she sighed out, still a little out of breath after the fit of laughter. "It's just... Tam, do you actually know anything about telepaths?"

Tamsin shook her head defensively. "I'm not training for Psi-Corps," she said. "I just know they're heavily regulated, and that most of them keep their abilities a secret to avoid prejudice." Or so that they could use them on unsuspecting friends, she thought murderously. Tamsin almost wished she could turn off her psi-blocker just so that Chandra could feel the strength of her anger, but she didn't dare. A Grade One telepath could probably stop her heart with a thought or something.

Chandra sat up a little straighter, her face now weary and just a little sad. "You have no idea how right you are," she said. "Look at you, Tam. You found out I was a telepath, and you... you thought that I would actually do that to her? Tam, I love her. More than I can say." She was angry, Tamsin realized. Quietly angry, nothing like the rage that Tamsin had displayed, but she was pissed.

"Oh, come on," Tamsin said. "What would you have thought? One of your best friends starts behaving oddly, and then you find out that her new lover is a Grade One telepath? How was I supposed to—"

Chandra cut her off with a loud, theatrical sigh. "Tamsin," she said, her voice sounding like a professor correcting a particularly inept student, "the grades of telepathic power go from one to one hundred." She narrowed her eyes as best she could. "Up."

Tamsin knew that expression. She grimaced, just a little, as she started to feel the righteous rage seep away to be replaced by mortified embarrassment. "So a Grade One is?"

"'Limited and or situational telepathic ability, of no significant degree,'" Chandra recited. "'Subject is allowed to self-monitor, conditional on results of personality profiling, but must make regular diagnostic visits to ensure that abilities are not increasing in scope or power.'"

Tamsin stood there for a long moment. "Oh," she said at last.

"I can do one thing, Tam," Chandra said. "It's tiny, so tiny that I barely even remember that I can do it most of the time. But when I finally worked up the guts to tell Gilly how I felt about her, and when she told me she felt the same way... " She blushed. "We've been playing with it a little," she admitted. "Just for fun, though. I would never do anything to hurt my Gillyflower." She reached over to where Gilly had managed to wriggle back into a sitting position and stroked the small of Gilly's back, causing her to shiver in bliss.

"Oh, God," Tamsin said, sitting down next to them. "I am so sorry, Chan. I just, I really thought..." She looked down at the floor, suddenly ashamed. "Can I, um, have a do-over on the last ten minutes?" she asked in a tiny voice.

Chandra reached over and patted her on the shoulder. She felt Gilly lean into her back, which would have been a lot more comforting if she didn't feel all four of Gilly's nipples pressing into her flesh. "It's okay, Tam," she said. "I won't lie, I'm still a little hurt, but... you really thought you were protecting Gilly. That goes a long way to making it right."

Gilly said, "It's my fault, too. I think I let us get a bit too carried away lately. But you know what they say, the mating urge is always strongest before second moulting." Gilly's species didn't really have a way with aphorisms, but everyone always thought it was too funny to tell her so.

"Even so," Tamsin said, "I want you to know I really am sorry. About everything." She hoped she sounded as sincere as she really was; she genuinely did feel terrible. Of course, some of that was the pounding headache that the psi-blocker caused, but...

"Forget it," Chandra said. "No harm done." She smiled, then winced at the movement of her own face. "Well, no harm done that I can't slap a medpatch on. Besides, you've done worse to me in Unarmed Combat. Remember the time you did the joint hold too hard and cracked my wrist? At least this time the instructor's not telling you what a good job you did."

Tamsin relaxed a little. "Okay," she said, lowering her voice conspiratorially. "I really am sorry I peeked, Chan, but now that I know, I really gotta know... Just between us, what exactly is your Grade One psionic talent?"

Gilly wriggled against her back. "It is sooo much fun!" she sighed out. "It definitely makes learning about deviant human sexual practices so much more enjoyable!"

"Oh, it's really minor," Chandra said modestly. "Barely worth mentioning." She smiled a crooked smile as she carefully avoided crinkling the left side of her face. "It's almost not even a psionic talent at all, really. You could probably learn how to do the same thing at a massage school."

Tamsin sighed. "This is how you're going to punish me for punching you in the face, isn't it?"

"Nah, I'm going to punish you for that by making you do my laundry for the next two weeks," Chandra replied cheekily. "By hand, too. The transporter beams always leave the fabric feeling too stiff. But this? This is just teasing."

"Oh, so not fair!" Tamsin cried out. "You are officially being cruel, Chan."

"Actually," Gilly said, "I think she is being entirely fair. The crime of physical violence alone might not merit such a punishment, but the crime of violating her personal privacy is the greater one, and doing her laundry by hand will give you ample time to meditate on the ethical implications of—"

"I, um, meant she's not being fair by teasing," Tamsin cut in. Gilly could probably go on for quite a while if you let her. "Come on, Chan, clue me in."

"Alright," Chandra said. "Take off the psi-blocker, and I'll show you." Tamsin must have given away the sudden surge of nervousness she felt somehow, because Chandra said, "I promise, it's nothing permanent or painful. You trust me, don't you?"

She said it lightly, but Tamsin knew exactly what she meant by the question. Words went only so far in making things right between them again. "Of course I do," she said, slipping the psi-blocker off of her head. She set it down on the floor. "Damn," she muttered. "I was really hoping the headache would go away when I took it off."

"Maybe I can help with that," Chandra said, reaching up and gently stroking Tamsin's temples. Amazingly, it did – Chandra's fingers felt wonderful, soothing away all the pain in a matter of moments. Tamsin's eyes fluttered just a bit as Chandra's soft touches worked their way down to brush at her cheek. "It's my talent," she said. "I can amplify pleasure. It only works when I'm in direct physical contact with another person, and I can't stimulate the pleasure centre of the brain directly, but I can make anything that feels good to them feel... better." She punctuated the words with a light caress of Tamsin's chin, and Tamsin was amazed at how good it felt.

"She did it to me for the first time when we made love," Gilly said softly in Tamsin's ear. The tickle of her breath against Tamsin's sensitive skin made her shiver in bliss. "I came so hard, Tamsin, it felt like a thousand fingers on my nipples and a thousand tongues on my clits. She made everything feel so good to me that I wanted to try everything. Do you understand now?"

"Yes," Tamsin husked out, arching her neck as Chandra's fingers danced their way along her throat. She closed her eyes for a long moment, enjoying that soft, gentle touch. It took a long time for her to focus them again properly when they opened. "I, um, I... " She tried to compose her thoughts, ask where this was going and what this would mean to their friendship, but just then Chandra traced the ridge of her collarbone and all she could think and say was, "Oh, fuck, Chan, it just feels so good... "

Chandra smiled at her, and Tamsin could see the arousal on her face. "Mmhmmm," she said, almost absently, as her fingers brushed at Tamsin's collar. They teased just lightly at the button, and Tamsin ached in anticipation, but Chandra didn't show any sign of getting ready to undo it. She was waiting, Tamsin realized. She was waiting for Tamsin to do it herself.

The moment Tamsin realized that, her fingers were fumbling at the buttons and zips of her cadet's uniform, removing it with more haste than speed. Her hands felt thick and clumsy, and she couldn't unfasten it anywhere near as fast as she wanted – mainly because with each button she undid, Chandra's fingers traced further down her quivering flesh. Behind her, she felt Gilly nuzzle her neck, and Gilly's rough tongue felt just as good as Chandra's fingers. Even better, perhaps. She felt like her nerves were all singing with pleasure now, and she could barely concentrate enough to pull her top off once she got to the last button.

It was worth the wait, though. Gilly's nipples felt like tiny vibrators where they rubbed up against the skin of her back, and Chandra's hands teased a moan out of Tamsin in seconds when they stroked her breasts. "Oh, oh God, oh, fucking yes," Tamsin moaned out, and she saw Chandra smile for just a moment before her eyes slipped shut. All her other senses were distant, unimportant now. There was only touch, only pleasure. Tamsin couldn't imagine caring about anything else.

She managed to slide her pants off before her hands reached out to touch Chandra, but only barely. It was so hard to stop herself. Everything felt so good now, even the way her hands glided over Chandra's soft skin. The different textures as she fondled Chandra's tight, firm nipples sent tiny starbursts of pleasure into Tamsin's brain, and she grunted in animal lust as Gilly gently slid out from behind her and she sagged down into the rough carpet. Even that felt so fucking good.

Then Chandra's hands were all over her, finding places to touch that felt... Tamsin's mind went warm and wet and red for a moment in bliss. It all felt so unbelievably fucking good. Gilly had wriggled around to lie next to her, pressing her body against Tamsin's and whispering in Tamsin's ear just how good it all felt, just how much she wanted it, just how long they'd waited to show it to her, and Tamsin realized somewhere around her second orgasm that this was why they'd let her walk in on them naked. Then she realized somewhere around her third orgasm that she'd already had two orgasms just from Chandra's touch.

Then Tamsin felt Chandra's tongue licking her clit, and that practically made Tamsin's brain shut down altogether. She couldn't even begin to focus on what Gilly was saying to her, not when every single nerve in her clit was having its own separate orgasm every time Chandra's tongue slid over it. She just melted into it all, and when Gilly straddled her face, she realized that even licking felt good now.

Tamsin lost track of time completely. Everything fell away, leaving behind only hot, sensual pleasure. She heard herself moaning into Gilly's vagina, but the sound had no meaning compared to the utter bliss of touch. Her legs spread wide to allow Chandra full access to every crevice of her womanhood, and her hands were stroking and her body was writhing and it all felt so good, it all felt so utterly fucking good...

She didn't even remember passing out. She only remembered waking up, groggy with free-floating endorphins and cuddled up to the warmth of her two friends. "Sorry," she said, her voice dazed with pleasure. "I think it was a little overwhelming."

"It's alright," Chandra said. "We fucked you so hard you lost consciousness. I'm taking it as a compliment."

Gilly pressed happily against her from the other side. "And now I have a sister pet!" she said enthusiastically. "I am so thrilled! There are so many things I wanted to do to Mistress that required more tongues and hands than I possess!"

Tamsin raised an eyebrow. "Um, 'sister pet'? I, um... I mean, I like this, but I don't know if I'm really... up for that, you know? I just—"

Chandra cut her off with a slow, gentle caress of her breasts that left her mewling in pleasure. "Please?" Chandra said, punctuating her words by tracing Tamsin's nipples. "Just give it a try, Tam, just for tonight. I think you'll really enjoy it, if you just give in and let yourself."

"I, um, I don't... " Tamsin felt her resistance melting away with every soft, stroking touch of Chandra's fingers. "Yes, Mistress," she whimpered out, and she was astonished at just how good those words felt on her lips.

"Good girl," Chandra said, and Tamsin quivered in pleasure at the way the words made her feel. "Good girl," she repeated, punctuating every word with a long, lazy, blissful caress that made it feel even better to give in.

The Permit

By David W. Landrum

Bryn slammed her fist on the table, her mouth open in disbelief, mind racing with questions, curses, and accusations. A communication had come across the screen informing her that the Station had postponed approval of her permit to open a new brothel. They had decided, it read, to 'review' the application – this after four months of benign assurances of its approval.

"We need another brothel," one of the officials in charge of approval had said, smiling sunnily. "We're past capacity. The existing establishments can no longer handle the customer load, and when that happens we start to get unauthorised prostitutes plying their trade, which causes serious problems."

Bryn had hired three women and brought them here, paying their expenses. She had rented space for her new business, shelled out endless fees for permits, advertised, and booked customers. She had almost depleted her funds. Now her project had landed in limbo.

She would ask Mitchell about it tonight.

Bryn went to Mulligan's, a bar she liked, for a drink. It was here she had turned her first trick on Station Shepherd. Sat at the bar, she thought, smiled, and got picked up. She caught no more customers that night, but the young man who paid her for it spread the word so that the next night she ended up on her back or on her knees for ten men. Normally she did not do that many, but she needed to make a name for herself and get some visibility. Bryn finished her drink, had another, and went for her appointment with Mitchell.

She liked Mitchell. A Terran of European descent from the Earth Alliance that operated the station, he had been around the block enough that Bryn let down her guard and enjoyed sex with him. She lay as he bore into her with a hard, even rhythm, grasping her tightly, rubbing his face against her cheek (once he had not shaved that day and chafed her face) as she flopped, wiggled, tightened her vagina, kicked, squealed, and purred.

It was the purring that made Terran men, and men from many other races of beings, seek out Mervogian women and pay high prices for their services. As far as Bryn knew, only her race had females who purred. Their throats vibrated and the vibration resonated through their bodies like the purring of a cat (cats were common to most planets in the Besrid sector of space, the races in that area kept them as pets and thought their purrs charming). Her purr had saved her life and enabled her to survive on Planet Lotus, the planet Space Station Alan Shepherd orbited.

Her husband, an army special forces operative, had run afoul of his commander officer, who got sent him on a mission that was in fact a trap. After his death, fearing he had told her something about the circumstances that led to the commander setting up him up to die, his commander gave Bryn three days to get out of Mervogian territory.

"Third day, if you're not out of the Federation, you're a dead woman. Tell anyone, especially the police, and I'll go after your family."

For the next three days she frantically prepared to leave. Everywhere she went, his agents shadowed her. Bryn finally got permission to settle on the Terran planet called Lotus Eyes of Lord Shiva. She had studied English in school and spoke it fairly well. Lotus would be a safe haven. It took all her money to get there and establish herself. In a dingy apartment, she sat alone watching the sunset on Lotus. Hungry, broke, she knew she had to rely on the only asset that remained to her. She had gone out, found where the prostitutes stood, and waited.

She put out until she could barely walk, made TD600.00 that night, and learned later most prostitutes charged

TD60.00 per trick, not TD100.00 as she had. Another working girl told her she fetched such a high prices due to her ability to purr. She remembered counting out her Terran Dollars, rejoicing that she would survive, and accepting the direction her life had taken.

Financially stable in only a short time, she got to know other sex workers who helped her learn the intricacies of working on Lotus. Prostitution was illegal there, so women volunteered to periodically service officials charged with enforcing the laws, Bryn included. A woman who ran an escort service eventually recruited her. After a dangerous, wearying year as a streetwalker, she became a high-class call girl, making ten times as much as when she sold herself on the sidewalks and alleys of Lotus's second largest city. Soon she accumulated enough money to start her own place.

The Space Station that circled the planet allowed prostitution. In fact, the sex industry thrived there. Mining employed thousands on Lotus, and miners came from distant worlds on one- or two-year contracts. Away from wives, they availed themselves of the legally available women on the space station. Several large brothers had located there and never lacked for customers. It seemed a good bet to Bryn, and everyone went well – until now.

As her mind returned to the bedroom and Mitchell, she decided to go for it. How long had it been? She lifted her rear up, squeezed, and let down all the layers of emotional protection she had created to distance herself from what she did for a living. After a moment, her purring grew louder than she ever remembered; then a spasm exploded though her body, filling her with bliss and ecstasy. She groaned, thrashed, and shouted. Her sudden orgasm set Mitchell off as well and he yelled and convulsed until they settled into silence. Bryn tapped his back, a signal she wanted him to climb off. He rolled over. After a long silence, he asked, "Did you actually come?"

"Of course I did. I am able to do that, you know."

"I know. I just thought you never did with customers; or you faked it. And that was not a fake."

"You're not just a customer. I think you can help me with something. You're a security officer here. I want to know why my permit is being held up."

"Oh, so that's the reason."

"The reason was I like you and I haven't got off in a long time. But if you appreciate me, you can give me an answer. It's not like I'm trying to get some top-secret something out of you."

Silence. Then he spoke.

"We're establishing a Mervogian consulate here. The head of their delegation is a Purie and doesn't like the industry. We can't and wouldn't want to close the brothels, but he was pretty pissed off when he found out you want to start one full of Mervogian women. And he didn't like the ads you're running."

Her ads on the adult TV channel had shown two cats and two of her women – the women in the buff, leaving nothing to the imagination. The caption beneath the cats read 'We purr.' The one next to the smiling naked women read, 'And so do we.' It had been an effective ad. Her site already had scores of customers signed up for opening day.

"So it's political."

"Yes."

Puries (followers of the Pure Land sect) were an ultra-religious political party that wielded a lot of clout on the Mervogian colony planets near the Station. Its influence did not prevail much on the Mervogian home worlds where Bryn had grown up, but a lot of colonists were adherents of Pure Land or at least felt favourably toward it.

"What can I do?"

"Ought to be obvious. Find someone in his delegation, fuck him, and blackmail him. He'll fight for your side then."

He stroked her pubic hair, something he liked to do. After a long silence, Bryn said, "That won't be as easy as it sounds."

***

Mitchell sent her files on all the members of the Mervogian delegation. None seemed like a good prospect. Her despair mounted. That evening she sat down with Avani, whom she had worked with as an escort girl on Lotus and who was visiting the station to see a relative. A beautiful, delicate Indian woman whose customers included many high-ranking officials on Lotus, she had been Bryn's closest friend in her days on that planet.

"You seem a little down," Avani observed.

"Worse than that," Bryn said, and she explained the situation. When she mentioned the name of the delegation's leader, Avani's eyes brightened with recognition.

"Avani, don't tell me – "

"It's not exactly what you're thinking. But he has a son who likes brown sugar."

Bryn knew the slang term for a prostitute of Indian descent from her days on Lotus. The European minority there used the term frequently. Indians were the predominant race in the Terran Alliance and Indian culture dominated that large, powerful political entity. She remembered her streetwalking days when she would smile or verbally offer her service to a passing group of European-descended Terrans and they would shout back, "Sorry, honey. We're looking for brown sugar." Indians didn't like the term and considered it racially demeaning – but what did that matter in the morally disconnected world of the sex industry?

"It wasn't me he hired," Avani said. "It was one of my girls. This kid is only about sixteen, but he has money and obviously disregards his father's morality."

"Then we can snare him."

"I think we can. If I remembered what Kamala told me, he's here now. Let's see what we can do."

The next day they found the young man standing in a crowd listening to speeches lauding the friendship of the Terran Alliance and the Mervogian Federation. Avani and Bryn filtered through the crowd and came near him. He glanced at Avani. She smiled.

"Conner, isn't it?"

He smiled. "Do I know you?"

"You know one of my employees. Kamala Kapoor."

Alarm lit his face. He looked around. After a moment, though, he seemed to calm.

"She's beautiful," he said. He spoke English well, as his father did. The delegation his father led came from Corita, a Mervogian colony planet near Terran space and surrounded by Terran and Rennet planets. Most of the people there could speak English.

"She can't be on the space station – they have her photo on the scanners and she's persona nom grata. But I'm here."

He leaned in close. "Too dangerous," he said with a gesture toward the podium where his father stood.

"This is my friend, Bryn," Avani said. "She's Mervogian."

His eyes lit with interest. Bryn immediately knew he was thinking about the ads she had run on the Station TV channel.

"Yes," she said, "Cats purr. So do I."

"I remember your advertisements. And, of course, I am a Mervogian, like you."

"There's a bar in the main concourse called Mulligans. The owner knows me – and he knows how to keep things private."

"I'll think about it."

"We'll see you there."

She and Avani turned to go.

They found a table in Mulligans. She explained the ad to Avani, who laughed.

"Very good. Do you think he'll show up?"

He did not show up.

The next day, the Council approved Bryn's permit.

Over the month that followed, she kept busy. Almost immediately she had to find new workers.

"We can't do this any longer," one of her women told her. She smiled tiredly. "Too many customers – even with you helping out."

Bryn had stepped out of her role as an escort to wealthier patrons like Mitchell and gone to work in the bedrooms of her new establishment, taking customers all day and into the night just as her employees did. They still could not keep up, which was not good for a beginning business. A rush trip to Corita enabled her to snare three new workers. Word soon got out and she hired five more Mervogian women from the surrounding area. Profits soared. Bryn went back to work as an escort, returning to her regular customers, who were glad to see her again. The first regular customer to whom she returned was Mitchell.

"You seem more practised," he grunted. He liked to carry on conversations while he fucked her.

"The last couple of months I pulled yeoman duty and worked with my other girls. I got a lot of practice in – like when I first started out and would turn fifteen tricks a night, she answered, voice tight with the lust she felt. Now shut up and fuck my pussy."

He obeyed, tightening his grip, pounding her so hard the bed shook. Bryn wanted to deny him the satisfaction of making her come, but she also wanted it. She lifted her legs, stuck them straight in the air, and purred in a long, low rhythm that matched his thrusting. Her breasts burned with passion. She sank into it. The orgasm engulfed him. She hoped she could have a second one, but he finished. It was enough. She could go for a second some other time.

After they had cleaned up, Mitchell opened his viewing port. Through the thick glass they could see the soft yellow sphere of Lotus. Phoebe, its single moon, hung above the planet's curve. As they looked on, the moon changed colours from red to purple to blue.

"You really don't know why the Council suddenly approved my permit?"

"I don't have a clue, Bryn. Honestly." He stroked the tuft between her legs. "I imagine you'll eventually find out."

Two months later an anonymous customer arranged to meet her on Lotus. She charged double (plus expenses) to do business there because of the possibility of arrest. When she entered the room at the luxury hotel, she saw Conner. He lay in bed with an Indian girl.

"Welcome," he said.

After their ménage a trios, he sent the Indian girl home. He and Bryn slept, woke, saw the sights of the capitol, and returned to the hotel (he had paid for a full twenty-four hours with her).

"I'll let you explain when you want to," she said as they had dinner in the hotel restaurant. "I'm sure you had something to do with it."

"What you and I and Kamala did was what I wanted to do with you and Avani the first time I met you. I was afraid my dad would find out. Then I realised it was time I stopped letting him control me. I told him the truth. He'd mentioned blocking your permit. I told him to stop or I'd go public with my propensity for women who practice your trade – which would not be good for his political career. He agreed, so I still keep my – shall we call them habits – to myself. Honesty is good in some cases, I suppose."

She smiled. "Thank you." After a pause, she said, "I have Avanti's number. She has to make herself scarce on Lotus because what we do is illegal down here. She owes me a lot of favours. I think if I called her up, she'd come over."

"She won't be busy?"

"She'll make time."

He smiled. Bryn felt gratitude and admired Conner's bravery. Why not give him what he wanted? She and Avanti had double-serviced men several times in the past. They had a routine down that seemed to please those willing to pay the money. Bryn decided they would do it for free this time. She would pay Avanti and not charge Conner. Something for something. She and Avanti would blend their skills at giving pleasure. He would be the recipient.

The most fortunate recipient, she thought.

Bryn called. Avanti said she would be there in an hour.

My First Alien

By Valerie Rose Hall

I had just finished a bubble bath and put on a nightgown. That'll become important later, the part about the nightgown. I crawled into bed with a book and started to read. It wasn't long before I fell asleep. I faintly heard the book fall to the floor as I drifted off to sleep.

I woke up in a much different room. It was like a mix of hospital and the living room of my aunt's log cabin. There was a wood-burning fireplace, comfy old couches and chairs, and a beat up wooden card table. If I could have shut off my other senses, the sight might have been pleasant. But it smelled like someone had tried to cover the fragrance of antiseptic with sawdust.

I felt strange sensations on my skin. I probed with my fingers and found that there were wires hooked up to me, stuck to my temples, my inner wrists, my breasts, and one trailing out of my nethers. I was naked. See, I told you that the nightgown was going to be important.

The most disconcerting thing was the creatures in the room. Two of them. The one that stood near me looked human, but it wasn't moving, not even breathing. One shadowy figure was sitting at the card table but I could see lights blinking on and off, like the table were a TV screen. Or a *computer* screen. Yes, I'm sure that it was a computer. It kept pressing buttons on it. This one definitely wasn't human.

Picture the stereotypical alien. Big grey head and small frail body. But its eyes were smaller and looked tiny on that large face. Its limbs were a little longer and leaner. And instead of light grey skin, it was almost black and looked like sleek rubber. It shone in the dim light of the room.

I should have been screaming for help. I should *at least* have been covering myself up. But I didn't. I was sort of drifting above myself, not really concerned. It was like watching a movie that starred someone who looked like me. I realized that I had been drugged.

Was that really an alien? Was I really in a log cabin? Or was this all a drug-induced hallucination?

The human figure came towards me. It didn't quite move right, not smooth and definitely not natural. The small jerks made me think of a robot, like Arnie in Terminator. It sat beside me on the couch. I could feel its warmth where its skin brushed against my foot.

Then there was a voice. It came from a speaker hidden in the ceiling somewhere. It sounded human, except its tones and inflections weren't quite right. It was trying to be a woman's voice, with a timbre smooth as silk, rich as cream. I guess that it was trying to be reassuring and comforting. But like everything else, it was off just a little bit. That didn't bug me, though, since this wasn't real.

"Good evening," the voice said. "I'd like to ask you a few questions and do a few tests. Do you consent?"

"Yeah, sure," I said. "Whatever you want is fine with me."

"Wonderful. What is your name? What is your age?"

The questions were basic things like that for a while, then it started asking me about my medical history. Was my heart okay. Any history of seizures. Stuff like that. It was like I was applying for a credit card or life insurance.

And that's when it got weird. Weirder. Whatever. It was all perfectly normal when it was happening.

The voice said, "My assistant Bob is going to touch you. Please tell me how his touches make you feel."

To this point, the human thing had been sitting still on the end of the couch. It didn't move, didn't adjust its position, didn't do any of the things that make humans human. But as I said, this all seemed normal at the time.

Bob turned towards me. His eyes were completely… alien. That's the only word I can think of. There was no spark of intelligence, no sign of emotion. Just a glassy stare. I shivered, disconcerted, even through the drug-like haze.

"Sure," I said.

His hand reached out and came to rest on my thigh.

"How does this make you feel?" the voice asked. There was still no inflection, no raising of her – or its – voice at the end of the sentence to indicate that it was a question. But I figured that it was a question, so I answered.

"A little warm," I said. "The hand is warm."

"Do you feel any emotions?" it asked.

"No. Maybe it's sort of nice, but that's it."

Bob moved his hand to my hip. "Do you feel any emotions?"

"No," I whispered. I was looking at his impassive expression, trying to tell if *he* felt any emotions.

He touched my breast, placed his fairly large hand over it, and asked me the question again.

"Hmm, maybe a little uncomfortable. I don't usually let strangers touch my lady parts."

"Interesting," he said. He moved his hand down and placed it atop my labia. I forestalled his question.

"Oh," I said. "Now that's a bit odd. I'm not used to men being so forward."

One finger poked out and worked its way inside me. I took in a shocked breath. Some part of me knew that this was wrong, that I shouldn't let this happen, but it didn't seem to matter.

"Hmm. It's weird. I'm not warmed up."

"Is that the only emotion you feel?"

"Let me think." I shifted around on the couch a little. The finger stayed perfectly immobile and I felt it rub against my insides as I moved. "That tickles a little."

The hand withdrew and Bob stood up. That's when I noticed that he was naked, and that he was very happy to see me. *Very* happy.

He took hold of my legs and repositioned me. One leg he draped over the back of the couch and the other he moved off so that my foot rested on the floor. I lay naked and wide open for him.

"Do you feel any emotions?" he asked as he stood over me.

I stared at his big cock. "Now there's confusion."

"Please explain."

"Well, I don't put out on the first date. Is this a date? I don't remember you taking me to dinner. But I'm really curious as to what you're hoping to accomplish with these questions. If you're trying to hit on me, you're not getting anywhere."

The voice didn't explain, didn't elaborate. The only response was Bob positioning himself above me, parallel, so that his large dick was hovering right in front of my wide open business.

"Do you feel any emotions?" the voice asked. Bob was holding himself up with his arms on either side of my head. His face was inches from mine but I felt no breath. I could see no twitches of his muscles.

"Mostly curiosity, now," I said.

"Please explain what has caused the change in your emotions."

"Well, I'm getting used to this odd situation. I'm actually pretty comfortable on this couch. That leaves curiosity. I want to know how far you are going to go with this."

He reached down and grabbed his dick, then wiggled it against my skin until it slid inside me. I wasn't ready, but he seemed to be coated with a lube or something similar because there was no friction or chafing. Then he asked the question for the last time.

"Still curious. Bob, are you going to have sex with me?"

"No, that is not within the parameters of this experiment. Thank you, Annie, you have been most helpful."

He withdrew and I fell asleep. Or was knocked out by something in the air. For whatever reason, I was unconscious again.

***

When I woke up, I was still in that room in the fake log cabin. My head felt a lot clearer. Some of the panic that I had been missing before crept in at the corners of my consciousness. But not enough to make me scream or run in terror. Just enough to bring my awareness into focus. That's when I decided that I wasn't dreaming or hallucinating.

I assume that I was supposed to have stayed unconscious until I was returned home. The aliens wouldn't have left me alone otherwise.

The wires were still hooked up to me. I took a brief moment to wonder if I would damage myself by removing them, then decided just to do it. They came off with a little pop. No pain or any sign of damage, thankfully. The one between my legs felt extremely weird coming out. Weird, and a little fun.

I stood up and looked around. The room was as I had last seen it, except that the two figures were gone. The first thing I did after that realization was to walk over to the table with the computer screen. It looked like an ordinary wooden table, at least until I touched it. A square of wood disintegrated and left me staring at a monitor. There were symbols in three colours on the screen. I didn't recognize any of them.

I explored for a bit. Whoever had made this room had done a fairly good job with the details. I could feel the wood grains under my feet. I could smell the ash from the fire. I could see the stars twinkling out the window. Or so I thought, until I got close enough to see that what was outside the window was a stage prop. A black curtain with holes poked through it to simulate a starry sky. An old Hollywood trick.

I tried to open the window, but it wouldn't budge. I ran to the nearest door. That's when I worried that I was naked. What if someone saw me? I grabbed one of the blankets off the back of the couch and wrapped it around myself like a toga. Then I opened the door to the alien ship.

Have you ever been on a navy ship? I took a tour of an old decommissioned destroyer many years ago. The corridors were barely wide enough for one person. There were bulkheads everywhere. And all the rooms were so small that I could touch opposite walls at the same time.

This had that same feel of closeness. But where there had been narrow ports everywhere on the warship, this had smooth, even walls. There were no rivets. There were no latches on the doors. There were no doors! The ceiling was one big panel of soft light. My eyes took a moment to adjust.

There was one of those monitors set in the wall beside the doorway that I had just exited. I looked at the screen. Behind the strange symbols, I could see a view of the room that I had just left, with the focus centred on the couch that I had lain upon. And along the walls of the hallway, I could make out more monitors. Curious, I went to see what scenes they would show.

The first one that I found showed a scene just like what I had experienced, except that the occupant on the couch was a man. He was being treated to some tender touching from a human-looking, large-breasted being, and he was obviously enjoying it. I moved on.

Each screen showed a scene more bizarre than the last. On the next, I saw two creatures, one whom I assumed to be human and one whom I assumed to be the one of the human-robots, going at it on a large bed. I studied the scene for a minute until I was sure that the man was the human and the woman was the robot. He was obviously more involved and was having his way with her. The woman wasn't moving her hips or her hands or her head. She might as well have been a blow up doll. The man didn't seem to care, though.

The next showed me a scene of a woman with a robot's arm buried fist-deep in her vagina. She was looking down at the arm, a curious expression on her face that would have mirrored my own during my test. But now it made me a little... tingly. Curious. Interested, even.

And so it went. There were a dozen tests in progress, and I saw various sexual experiments. Some were boring, either because of what was happening or because the subjects were not engaged in the event. Some made my heart race. There was one room with two women which I watched for a moment out of curiosity, and one room with a man giving head to another man, which gave me a new rush. In both cases, I couldn't tell which one was the robot.

I'll tell you the details about the last scene that I encountered, at the end of the hallway. It was the most memorable one. The final monitor showed me something that would not have been possible for humans. There was a woman lying on a couch, which was a sight that I was now used to. The figure that stood above her was human except that it had two penises, one above the other. That alone made blood rush through my body.

The man – whom I assumed to be another robot by the way it moved and based on its inhuman anatomy – moved closer to the woman, who had her legs spread apart and her butt propped into the air. The man moved towards her. He guided one penis into her pussy and the other into her butt. She tipped her head back and opened her mouth. The man started moving back and forth, pushing those two cocks into her again and again.

She was definitely into it. She squirmed around on the couch, swayed her hips side to side to get as much feeling as she could. Her hands cupped and squeezed her breasts and her fingers rolled her nipples back and forth. This was the first human woman I had seen who was fully engaged in the experiment. I would have been, too.

I watched the whole show. A combination of curiosity and, I'm not ashamed to admit, arousal kept me there, spying like a teenager who found a peephole into the girls' change room. And like that horny teenager, I was touching myself while I watched. I imagined what it would feel like to be taken in the pussy and ass at the same time. I had two fingers on my clit which I slid inside my pussy. I was just reaching for my ass with my other hand when the show ended.

The end was sudden. The man went from vigorous thrusting to withdrawal without a break. I couldn't tell if either person had reached orgasm. I hadn't, and I was left feeling unfulfilled. The man walked out of view of the camera and the woman fell unconscious.

With nothing else to do and nothing new to see, I returned to my room.

The black alien was there. And he was freaking out. With wild gestures, he swung his arms around, looking around the room in a panic. He sort of ran and hopped simultaneously, moving around the room and then to the computer screen. After a few taps, he threw out his arms again and ran-hopped some more. For an alien species, they at least knew what a good human freak-out looked like.

I stepped in and the door closed itself after me. The sound of it sealing caught the alien's attention.

His head snapped around and locked on to me. I saw relief wash over him. His body relaxed and he stopped his frantic motions. Some emotions are universal, it seems. I'd soon discover another that was universal.

"Bob, are you looking for me?"

He stared at me, then blinked. Then he pointed at the couch.

"I'm not tired," I said. "And I don't want to get gassed again." I started to saunter towards him and I let the blanket slip from my body. I pushed my breasts forward. I had no idea if he would respond to my advance, but it certainly couldn't hurt. Why would they be studying sex if they weren't interested in it?

"I saw some very exciting things going on out there," I said and gestured towards the door. Did he understand me? He stood still as I approached.

I made my voice velvety smooth. "Why are you doing this? Are you interested in human women? Have you ever had sex with a human?" No reaction from him. "*Can* you have sex with us?"

Maybe he understood, maybe he didn't. In either case, his body reacted to me.

From between his long, slender legs I saw something emerge. It grew until it was half a foot long and wide, so wide. The alien's cock was as black and sleek as the rest of his body, except for the head, which looked like a pink mushroom. How good would those wide glans feel passing into me?

"I thought so," I said. "I knew that's what you wanted."

The alien stood rooted in place as I reached him. I got

down on my knees in front of him and took hold of his dick. He turned his head down to watch me. I could feel the pulse of his heart through the blood vessels. There was a slightly earthy scent mixed with a chemical odour coming from it. Odd, but appealing. When looking back on the experience, I would wonder if the smell included pheromones. That might explain why I was so eager to taste it.

I put my lips around the head. The skin had the consistency of rubber but was glossy like it had a thin coating of oil. He would never need to use lube. It tasted as appealing as it had smelled.

As I took him, the alien finally reacted. I heard an intake of breath and I could feel tremors as his legs shook.

He slid so easily in and out of my mouth. I moved my head up and down on his big black cock, so much like a human's. I wouldn't wonder about that again until days later. At the time, I had only one thought in my mind.

I played my tongue over the glans, circled around it, as I stroked his shaft with my hand. I felt a shudder course through his body. Knowing that I was giving him pleasure filled me with joy and enticed me to continue. There was a need to continue, to bring him to the edge and beyond.

My lips folded over his head and I licked the tip of his cock. His earthy scent filled my nose and it was intoxicating. I moved my head down, took as much of him as I could. I suppressed a gag as the tip touched the back of my throat. Over and over again I slid my lips along his shaft.

His hands, long and slender fingers, wrapped into my hair and held on. Some of my long blonde locks were falling across my face, tickling his cock as they brushed against it.

I felt his legs and arms tense up and knew that he was ready. I pulled back slightly, only taking him halfway into my mouth, and grabbed his shaft again and pumped it with quick and powerful strokes, right down to the base. He let out a low-pitched cry and came.

The hot cum spurt into me. I swallowed once, twice, as he poured himself out. Then he drew away from me and his cock slipped out from between my lips. A little bit of his brown fluid dripped from the tip onto the floor.

He put his hands up, a gesture that I took to mean 'stop'. His eyes were wide again.

"What's wrong? Isn't that what you wanted?"

He was still hard. Was that normal for their species?

I backed away, but I held out a hand, palm up, as an invitation for him to follow me. I backed up until I bumped into the couch.

The alien let out a series of noises. I can't even remember what they sounded like. Clicks or chirps maybe. I couldn't understand him just as he couldn't understand me. The voice that had spoken to me during the test must have been synthesized specifically for the experiment.

"Come," I said. I lay on the couch and put my legs into the same position that the human robot, Bob, had put me in during the test. One leg over the back of the couch, one on the floor, pussy proudly displayed for everyone to see. "This is what you really want, isn't it? So do I. Come take it."

Whatever had been holding him back released its grip and the alien stepped forward slowly, as if unsure of himself. When he finally reached my side, I took his slender hand and interlaced my fingers with his. Six fingers per hand, I noticed for the first time. I tugged on him, trying to coax him into lying atop me. He was still fully erect.

I started rubbing myself, spreading my juices out and lubricating my pussy lips. Each time I brushed against my clit, I felt a jolt run up my spine. He watched my show. I saw a battle raging in his eyes.

"Fuck me, whoever you are," I whispered. My eyes were locked in his. The battle was over, and all I saw there now was lust. "Fuck me and I'll tell you how good it makes me feel."

He moved above me and slid his dick into my waiting hole. He was still wet with my spit and I was more than ready, eager to accept him. He slid in and started moving back and forth, back and forth, slowly building up the rhythm.

"That feels great," I said. "Keep going, just like that."

He had stamina. He fucked me slowly for a long, long time. I couldn't even guess how long it lasted. In and out, over and over again, drawing himself back until his head was at my lips, sliding it back in again to fill me up. That mushroom-shaped head felt amazing as it passed through my opening again and again.

His expression, alien as it was, was still clearly one of excitement and joy. His small almond-shaped eyes were wide and sparkled in the dim light of the room. His thin lips were turned up at the sides and were parted slightly. His hands were on my shoulders and it was the most tender sensation a lover had ever given me.

I closed my eyes and relaxed and smiled. I wrapped my hands around his back and let his slow motions carry me away. I imagined myself a wave in the ocean, slowly gliding up the shore, then back into the greater body of water, over and over, constant and peaceful and wonderful.

After a blissful eternity, he started to increase his pace. It was a constant, steady, and agonizingly slow build-up. Now I just wanted him to ravage me, pound me hard and fast and make me come all over him.

After the most intense build-up I'd ever had, he had finally reached a furious, frantic thrusting. He drilled me hard and fast, like I had been longing for. His hands closed on my breasts and I felt like I would burst. My whole body was on fire, burning from the intense pleasure that was spreading out from my pussy like a blast furnace.

He was wonderful. He was amazing.

The pace grew quicker. I don't know how he did it. It was inhuman. He kept going faster and faster. I looked at him and saw his features lost in a blur of motion. His hands held on tight to my tits; they were the only part of him that I could focus on.

But I could not hold my focus any longer. His speed was incredible. The pure pleasure that he brought out of me was beyond overwhelming. My vision blurred and my eyes watered. I couldn't breathe for the intensity of it.

It felt like his dick was filling me up completely, never leaving, while at the same time it was moving across my flesh so fast that it kept every nerve constantly firing. My brain couldn't handle the sensation. I had no idea what was happening, or how long it lasted, or where I was, or who I was.

My orgasm was more intense than anything that I had ever felt. I surged up off the couch, pushed the alien up with me. My pussy clenched his huge cock in its grip, squeezed him until he, too, reached orgasm.

His cum erupted into me. I could hardly feel it. My flesh was turning numb after having been constantly stimulated for God only knows how long. When we were both finished, I collapsed and finally started breathing again. I sucked in huge gulps of air. The alien was also panting, but he recovered much faster than I.

All I could do was look at him as my mind tried to sort out what had just happened and bring me back to some semblance of coherence.

He got up and stumbled over to the computer console. After a minute of tapping at the screen, the female voice flowed into the room.

"Can you describe your emotions for me?" it asked. Then, with almost a hesitation, "Was it good for you, too?"

"Yes," I whispered. "It was incredible. The best I've ever had."

"Please elaborate," she said.

"I can't even begin. It all felt so wonderful. It's like I'm high, like I'm floating. I can't feel my body and I don't care. How did you go so fast? That was magnificent."

"Thank you for your participation."

I made eye contact with the alien one more time before I lost consciousness. The last thing I remember from the alien ship is a look of bliss on that alien face. It was a look that must have mirrored my own.

I woke up in my own bed, in my own house, with pure yellow sunlight angling in through my own window. I slowly opened my eyes. All of the images from the night were crowding in the forefront of my mind, clamouring for attention. I briefly wondered if it had been a dream, but dismissed the possibility. The memories were too vivid, too pure. None of them were fading away, like dream memories always do. I was sore between the legs, rubbed raw. And my nightgown was nowhere to be found. I assume that the alien kept it as a memento.

It had been real. I'm as sure of that as I am of my own existence. I've never had sex that good before or since. I desperately hope that my first alien lover is not my last.

Hot Summer

By Myriam Stommel and Mirren Hogan

Summer, contrary to the gentle warmth of her name, stormed out of the hydroponics bay, her face pink and furious. Her hands were curled into tight fists as if she was ready to pound them into someone. In truth, she only wanted to use them on her boss. Just because she was a master, didn't mean she was right about everything. What did old people know anyway? Fucking bitch!

Kell was equally storming, just for entirely different reasons, and towards the space station's infirmary. His forearm was decorated with a long gash that was bleeding profusely, just because his idiot of a wingmate was too stupid to handle a knife at the lunch table. Cursing all the way, Kell stomped past the entrance to the hydroponics bay, not even taking notice of anybody crossing his path.

She saw him at the last moment and swerved to avoid a collision. "Watch where you're fucking going!" she snapped.

"Watch your mouth, you fardling little brat!" Kell growled. His instinctive reaction of putting out his arm to ward her off resulted in him smearing some blood on her. "Now get out of my way, drone."

"Drone?" Her face went from pink to red. "Do I look like a drone? Oaf!" She grimaced and wiped his blood off her arm and onto her apprentice clothes.

"With that language you sure sound like one!" he hissed, dripping blood. He snorted and stormed on. "Fucking little bitch!"

"Then you're as stupid as you are blind!" she called out after him, then cursed under her breath that she was going the same way.

"That'd be your trademark, not mine," Kell growled back

at her. Suddenly he stopped when he noticed she was still behind him, walking in the same direction. "Are you following me now?" he challenged. "What the hell do you want?!"

She snorted. "Right, like I don't have better things to do than follow you! Besides which, there are better views around here than your ass!" Strictly speaking that wasn't necessarily true. She stormed past him so she was now walking in front.

"Oh, so you say, Miss Drone, and put your ass in my face!" He sped up to pass her again, not accepting being left behind and insulted by a little brat.

"My ass is better than yours, crap for brains!" she called back. She was starting to enjoy this, it was therapeutic, taking her frustration out on someone else.

"If you can even call that an ass... there's nothing there. Nothing worth touching anyway." He pulled up beside her, looking her up and down. "Nothing in the front either... peas on a board at best." He snorted. "How old are you? Ten? Twelve?"

"18. I bet my tits are bigger than your dick!"

"Prove it," he returned calmly, a smug grin on his face.

She laughed. "Yeah, keep dreaming. Besides. I'd hate to humiliate you!" Her tone was clearly sarcastic.

"Yeah well... your puny titties are definitely not a dream – unless I'm having a nightmare... " Kell chuckled now. "Besides, you made the claim, so you've got something to prove." How far was it still to the infirmary? "Come on, humiliate me. Unless of course you're afraid your peas don't measure up to my dinky dick... "

"There's no need, your admission of how small you are is it quite enough for me." She grinned.

"So you are afraid." He grinned back. "Besides... I never

even bragged about the size of my dick. That was you, claiming to have the milk production facilities of a genetically modified cow." He swayed then, ever so slightly, but it caused him to nearly mis-step. He raised his arm and cradled it in his other hand, pushing on toward the infirmary.

"I never claimed that, I just said they were bigger than your... " She frowned. "Not that I give a fuck, but you don't look so good. Maybe you should hurry up while you still have blood left."

"Ah hah! You're changing the subject," Kell said triumphantly though pale. Once challenged he would not back down – even though this was more banter than battle. However, he was starting to feel a little dizzy... "Fardling dung brain," he muttered again, wanting to plant his foot in his idiot wingmate's face for the umpteenth time for being so fucking stupid with the knife. "Ahh... fucking hell – look at this mess." He looked down at himself to inspect the bloody spots on his clothes.

"That's going to take some scrubbing to get out," she agreed. "Maybe you should tie something around that to stop the bleeding while you walk." She shrugged. "Or don't. Whatever."

"I did... have something..." He frowned. "Must've lost it... " He looked back the way he came, but saw nothing. And while fury had kept him going this far, the girl had worked off the steam and turned his anger to amusement – and now, his vision blurred and narrowed into tunnel vision. "I have to sit down... now." And he plopped to the ground.

She stood and looked down at him. "Oh come on, it's not that bad. Just a scratch really. I say you're fine."

He laughed, masking the nausea that was clawing his insides. "Come on, help me up. I feel kinda... heavy... though light... " He blinked and pointedly looked away from his bloodied arm, trying to cover the nasty gash with something, anything.

She made a sound of disbelief. "Yeah, you need my help. And dragons are all pink and purple. The next thing you'll say is that you're hung like one." In spite of that, she leaned over and hooked her hand under his and tugged.

"Of course I am… but you wouldn't believe it." He struggled up with her help, and since fate is a bitch, he lost his balance and stumbled forward into her chest to face plant between her so-much-talked-about breasts. "I totally did that on purpose," he muttered, muffled by her body.

She froze. "Of course you did," She put her hands on his shoulders and took a step back so he wouldn't face plant on the ground – however tempting that was. "Come on, stop being a big wuss."

"I've been called a lot," Kell burst out indignantly, "asswipe, toe rag, turd head, drone brain, tunnel-snake – but never a wuss!" His silver-green eyes narrowed on her, because her rather lovely visage was inexplicably blurry before him. "Alright… get me to the infirmary. You're hazy… "

"There's a first time for everything," she pointed out. "Come on then drone brain, it's not that far anyway." She held on to his upper arm – quite muscular, she noted – and lead him forward slowly. "So who did you piss off?"

"Why would you say that?" Again the tone of indignation. He leaned on the girl, who was not at all just peas on a board, as his face had discovered earlier when he had stumbled into her.

"Just call it a hunch," she replied. "Don't tell me, you tried to steal someone else's woman, and they didn't like it and stabbed your arm? Or a boy didn't welcome your advances?" She grinned.

"Not even half as dramatic," Kell grunted. "Just an idiot wingmate who shouldn't be allowed to eat with fork and knife. Spoons only." They arrived at the infirmary. "Besides, I just like coming here and have the cute healers take care of me."

"Good luck finding one. All the cute healers are working with animals," she replied with a shrug. "Here you are. In one piece, mostly. Can you walk in by yourself, or do I have to put you to bed?"

"I wouldn't mind that, actually," Kell said. Then he spotted a good-looking kid about his age. "Or I can ask him. If he tells me he's a vet, I'm gonna tell him I'm a horse stud and need my balls scratched." He laughed, then winced. "Fuck… that hurts," he hissed and clamped his arm, not looking at it.

"He doesn't look like a vet to me," she commented. "Wrong clothes for one thing. And he doesn't look dumb enough to fall for the crap about you being a horse. Unless you mean the kind that runs messages across the planet. I doubt you'd last five minutes doing that unless you were chasing tail."

"I'm always chasing tail," Kell said. "Unless I'm bleeding to death." He sat down, nausea churning in the pit of his stomach. "A little help here!" he shouted at the healer. "And now would be a good time, too!"

The healer rolled his eyes. "Keep your pants on." He walked over and looked down at Kell's arm. "Who did you piss off this time?"

Summer laughed.

The healer wiggled his eyebrows at her and then leaned in to take a closer look. "The good news is you're going to live. You may need a couple of stitches though."

"Stitches?" Kell quickly cleared his throat to cover the hysterical hitch in his voice. "Fuck it! Can't you do anything else?"

"I can amputate your arm, but that seems a tad extreme to me. Hold on while I get the saw." The healer pretended to step away.

Summer was laughing so hard she had tears in her eyes.

"Just fucking cut the crap and get this fixed!" Kell suddenly exploded at the healer. "And you, shut the fuck up, brat!" he spat at Summer. "Get out! You're not needed anymore!" He felt ready to throw up, but like hell he would be that weak in front of those two, in front of anybody for that matter!

"I was trying to," the healer pointed out. "Wait there, I need a basin of water. And you," he addressed Summer, "had better stay in case he... takes a turn for the worse." Fainted in other words.

"Oh good," she said when the healer was out of hearing range. "Babysitting for an ungrateful fucking ass, just what I need. As if I don't have more important things to do."

"Then fardling go and do them," Kell snarled, ungrateful indeed.

"I'll stay, because the healer asked nicely, fuckwit," she retorted. "And no I don't do nappies or breastfeed!"

"I'd rather suck dick than touch your puny titties!" Kell spat.

"Which speaks volumes about your lack of good taste," she retorted.

Not true, he'd much rather suckle on her supple breasts, but he would not admit that. "Why are you still here?!"

"I'm watching you in case you faint, remember? Big baby."

He snorted. "So unnecessary. Why don't you do something useful instead? Like getting me some water."

"Only if I can drown you with it." She did see a cup and a jug so she poured him a cup. "Here." She offered him the drink.

Kell grabbed the cup like a man dying of thirst, his hand shaking and almost spilling the precious water. At least it was cold, ice cold, and fresh. But it felt like it was too little too late. He swallowed repeatedly, desperately trying to keep the contents of his stomach down. There was just too much blood dripping from his arm for his taste.

Just then, the healer returned. He handed the basin of water to Summer. "Hold this for me, would you? Right now Kell, hold out your arm." He washed it down carefully and then applied two stitches and a bandage quickly so the shuttle pilot wouldn't have time to complain.

"There, all done and good as new," he said, stepping back.

"If wrapped up is how he started," Summer pointed out.

"Yes, well..."

Kell's breathing normalised then. The healer had been done before he could even react to the stitching. He had to admit, at least inwardly, that the healer knew what he was doing. He glanced at the young man appreciatively, but returned to a sneer before he could be called out on it. "It'll do, I suppose," he said dismissively. The churning in his stomach ebbing away, Kell felt safe to get up, but swayed slightly, still feeling somewhat light-headed.

The healer ignored his attitude. "Maybe you should get some rest," he suggested, taking the basin back from Summer.

"Good idea, great reason to miss wing practice," Kell snorted, then turned to Summer. "Where are your quarters? Might as well work on this... sexual tension we have going here, babe." Yeah... he was back to normal, alright.

"I could use a good laugh," she answered tartly. "I just can't wait to see how small it is!" She started out the exit without bothering to see if he was behind her.

"Let's do it then," Kell challenged. "Unless you're scared

that the puny titties don't measure up to the dinky dick after all?" He laughed and walked out behind her.

"I have far less to worry about than you do," she snapped over her shoulder. Except that she should be in an apprentice class. To fuck with that though. She kept walking until she reached the apprentice quarters which were deserted at that time of day.

"I don't worry about anything, ever," Kell said nonchalantly. "Waste of time. Fighting, sex, and flying a shuttle – and all three at the same time, now that's worth spending time and energy on." He'd followed her all the way and caught up to her just as she was about to enter the living quarters, cutting her off with one arm across the doorway as he leaned with one hand against the doorframe on the opposite side of where he stood. "So, how about it?" He grinned openly at her now, a challenge clear on his handsome features and in his sparkling silver-green eyes.

"You really think you can live up to your own hype, hmmm?" She tilted her head to the side slightly.

He feigned surprise. "What hype? I'm not the one full of myself." He grinned again. "As I recall, you claimed peas to be bigger than the dragon." He wiggled his eyebrows at her.

"I did not, you big oaf." She went to duck under his arm.

"Did too," he shot back, dropping his arm and catching her around her waist.

She squirmed but only ended up facing him, her eyes flashing. "Go on, impress me then," she challenged.

"Who cares if you're impressed?" Kell shrugged, the gesture serving just fine to pull her closer. "You tickled the dragon, you're gonna feed it." His head dipped and he buried his face at the crook of her neck, tasting her just behind her ear, his fashionable three day stubble probably tickling her. "You can brag about it later."

"And who says I want it?" she asked, sounding snappish but making no effort to move away.

Kell tilted his head back to look at her. "You're not scratching my eyes out... yet." He gave a low, throaty laugh and made a hissing sound while mock-clawing with his free hand at her face. "I guess I'd better watch out though," he murmured then, nuzzling her neck again. "You sure are a feisty one." Slowly he pushed her backward so that they ended up in the hallway.

"Maybe I don't scratch," she suggested breathlessly. "Maybe I prefer to bite." She was trying to keep her balance while walking backward, frustrated that she grabbed his arm to keep herself upright.

"Oohhh – bite marks, huh." Kell practically purred at that. "The battle scars of a lover. I have a few of those... " He nibbled her earlobe. "Where are your quarters?"

"Right behind me," she said, turning her head just enough to see. "You'd better watch out, I might bite harder than you think."

Kell just laughed as he guided her into her quarters and shoved the door shut. "If you bite harder than you bark, I'll be more than happy."

"Shut the fuck up," she turned them around, put her hands on his chest and pushed him against the door, then started working on the buttons on his shirt, undoing them until she could push his shirt off his shoulders and down his arms.

Kell let himself be pushed back even though he usually was the one pushing. But shells, this one was feisty! And she already had him at full attention. "What," he breathed, "no more insults?" His large hands cupped her breasts and pushed them up so he could nuzzle her cleavage down the neckline of her tunic.

"Not yet," she replied, but then his shirt did have to come down past his bandage, and she wasn't gentle in the effort.

"Yeow, bitch," Kell growled. "Just say you want me naked, don't kill me in the process." He dropped his arms long enough for the shirt to slide down and fall to the floor, before his hands returned to her breasts, this time under the tunic.

She grinned maliciously. "Stop being a wuss." She moved forward and pressed her lips against his chest, kissing and nibbling his skin. If he wanted bite marks, he was going to get them.

"Oh, here we go, the insults are back... " Kell groaned and quivered at her touch – and the feel of her skin under his hands. He kneaded her breasts, teasing her nipples and rolling them between his fingers. "Nice peas... " he breathed.

She wasn't going to take that insult. She moved her mouth down to one of his nipples, circled it a time or two with her tongue and then took it between her teeth and bit down on it.

"Oh fuck... " Kell grunted as the sensation shot from his chest right down into his groin. It was the perfect mixture of pleasure and pain, and inadvertently his fingers twitched and squeezed down on her nipples in return.

She hissed through her teeth and bit harder. Truthfully, she'd never been with anyone who made her feel half as excited. She reached down with her hands and brought them around so she could start on undoing his belt.

Another groan deep in his throat, and Kell moved his hands up, prying Summer's face away from his chest. His head dipped low and he captured her mouth in a hungry, forceful, almost brutal kiss. "Hell – he murmured between gasps, "you taste better than you look... "

"Fuck you," she retorted, responding to his kisses in kind. She worked his belt loose, undid his trousers, and pushed them down as far as her arms could reach while standing.

As soon as she was done with that, off came her tunic, while he stepped out of his pants pooling around his ankles on the floor. "You will," he growled, bearing down on her mouth, chin, jawline, neck, earlobe, and mouth again. His hands were scraping and teasing her smooth skin as they moved over her body. Then his fingers got hold of the waistband of her trousers and pushed it down so he could cup her buttocks, while pressing her close to his body.

She managed to kick her ankles free of her trousers and wrapped her arms around his neck, her palms pressed against his shoulders. She dug her nails into his skin, getting more and more swept away in the moment. Her breathing was so heavy each exhale was more a moan than a breath. She was done with insults, at least for now, instead saving her breath to say, "Fuck me."

Kell groaned and his erection literally twitched at those words. "Ohh I will... " he said between clenched teeth. His back arched as she dug her nails in, and his hands, squeezing her buttocks tightly, lifted her clear off the ground. This put her in a position where she could wrap her legs around him, although she wasn't sure he'd be strong enough to hold her weight.

Her move opened her up invitingly, temptingly, bringing her hot centre right on top of his straining cock. He could feel her heat, her wetness. Kell grunted and turned, almost forcefully slamming her back against the solid wood door. He nuzzled his face between her breasts, licking and nipping the soft mounds and hard nipples – and then sharply grazed her skin with his teeth as he plunged into her, burying himself deep inside her.

She was momentarily winded as her back slammed into the door and everything went hazy. She smiled and shook her head to clear it. He certainly knew how to play, just the way she liked it. She pushed her chest forward, enjoying the feel of his mouth on her breasts. It hurt, but not quite enough, until he slammed into her with enough force to take her breath away again. Her back arched, and she cried out in pleasure and pain. Her cry was loud enough to carry throughout the quarters had anyone been there to hear it.

Her cry only served to egg him on. "You like that, little bitch?" He grunted as he thrust into her again, pulling her down on him with his large hands firmly on her hips. His face pushed into the crook of her neck, then returned to her breasts, lips and tongue tasting the salt on her skin. The tension in his cock, in his body was building as he slammed into her, again and again. "Come on, bitch," he gasped, "tighten up!"

"Maybe… " she said, speaking a word with every thrust, "you… should… have… been… bigger!" Although, she was suitably impressed with his size. She clenched her muscles around him as her nails dug in tighter, raking his back. She had every intention of leaving marks on him. He wouldn't be forgetting her in a hurry.

"Hah!" He grunted as she clamped down on him. He drove on, faster now. "Maybe… you shouldn't… have been… fuckin' around… so much," he growled with each thrust, her hot, wet, tight but oh-so-slick insides stroking his cock rigorously. The delicious burning sensation of sweat biting into the scratch marks she was leaving on his back added a wicked fuel to the fire.

"Maybe… if you… stayed… out of… boy's… asses… you would… know… how… a… woman… should… feel!" she retorted. She felt her excitement building toward its peak. She moaned loudly, "Y… e… s… " she panted. She moaned again as she climaxed, not caring who in the Station heard.

"Woman! Pah!" he spat, which turned to an animalistic roar when the tension in his cock exploded as she clenched furiously on him in her own climax and he spilled himself inside her. "Yeeaahhh!" And his teeth sunk into the soft part between her neck and shoulder, actually nicking the skin to draw blood. For a long moment he leaned heavily into her, pressing her hard against the door, body trembling in the aftershocks of his orgasm while she was literally milking him. He panted, hot breath fanning the blonde curly hair at her ear. "Not fuckin' bad," he admitted breathlessly finally, already a smug grin back on his face.

"Of course it wasn't," she replied as if it was a given. She leaned forward so her head rested on his shoulder in a gesture of momentary exhaustion, not intimacy. She hurt inside and out, but she'd never felt so good. She waited until her breathing returned to normal and then lowered her legs back to the ground. "Now get the fuck out. I have things to do."

"Meeow!" Kell mock-clawed at her and hissed, then he laughed and grabbed some cloth that was lying around (he didn't even care if it was rag, towel or shirt) and cleaned himself off before pulling on his pants. "I'll be calling you when I get bored of nice and tight boy asses," he said smugly and grabbed his shirt, not bothering to put it on. Quickly, not leaving her any time to react, he grabbed her by the back of her neck, pulled her close and robbed her of one more rough and ready kiss before backing out the door.

She didn't even look as he left, she just grabbed her robe and headed toward the bathing area. She was going to need a long soak after that.

Drip

By Jeremy M. Gottwig

"**W**ater, water everywhere," Lorn mumbled. He took a sip and returned the tin cup to the centre of the table. "And not a drop to drink."

"You're a true poet," commended Ralia.

"They aren't my words."

"Well, I like the way you say them." Ralia submerged a fingertip into the cup and withdrew a droplet. The flickering candlelight turned the liquid into a jewel. She rolled the water over her cracked lips.

"Drink. Don't waste it."

Ralia frowned but didn't respond. She never wasted anything.

A breeze nudged their torn curtain and twisted through the hovel. Ralia glanced at the window and caught a hint of stars peering through the twilight. It would be dark soon, but she didn't want to think about that now. She intended to force this day deep into night.

Lorn looked away, but Ralia, leaning across the table, kissed him. The sting of his lips against hers stole her breath. She winced and withdrew, but the sensation lingered.

"I'll miss you," Ralia whispered.

Lorn nudged the cup in her direction. "Finish it," he said.

"You first." Ralia forced a smile. Despite the dryness in the back of her throat, she would not drink the last of their water. Lorn would be traveling tomorrow to find more. Ralia worried that this time he might not return.

"I want you to finish it."

Ralia heard distant thunder, but she knew there would be no rain. "I won't," she insisted.

A blast of dusty wind angered their candle. Lorn shielded the flame. Ralia could hear the irradiated water of the lake brush along the dead shore.

Poison water.

They sat in silence as twilight faded into night. The cup waited between them, their last gulp of fresh water, untouched.

Lorn broke the spell. "Drink it. Please."

Ralia sighed and stood. She turned her back to him. "Untie me," she said. She felt one hand on her arm while his other pulled the bow knot loose around her neck. Her faded red dress slipped off her shoulders and gathered around her feet. She wore nothing underneath. Lorn ran a hand down her spine and brought his lips to her skin.

Ralia pulled away and took the cup. She had wanted him to bring the last of their water on his journey, but he would have none of it. They would drink it together, he had insisted, or he would go without.

Ralia moved to their thin mattress on the floor. Lorn held back. Ralia could almost feel his eyes. "It will go to waste," she said as she extended herself over the mattress. She took the last of their water and spilled it between her breasts. The cool liquid started down her breastbone and gathered at her bellybutton. Lorn rushed to her and sucked the water off her skin before it spilled into the fabric. Ralia laughed.

Lorn kissed her. The water drizzled from his mouth into hers.

Ralia swallowed. Her body gave her no choice.

"That was careless," Lorn whispered, but by then his breath had turned heavy. His coarse hands circled her waist and moved into her inner thighs.

"Don't go," Ralia begged as her body took over. It was something she had desired to say throughout the day.

"I'll stay," Lorn whispered.

Ralia let her imagination drown in the fantasy. "You'll stay," she said. She forced down his trousers and rolled on top of him. Lorn licked his hand and moistened the lips between her legs. "Don't... " she said, but the fantasy carried her cautions away. Lorn rolled his hands over her hair, her breasts, her backside. Ralia barely noticed as she moved her body against his. Colours flashed across her vision. "You'll stay," she said. "You'll stay."

Morning came. Ralia woke alone. The sunlight glared at her through their small window. The curtains lay on the floor, as if the wind had kicked them off during the night. Ralia remained in bed, uncovered, until she heard voices in the distance. She grabbed her rifle and propped it next to the window.

And then she waited.

Clurichaun

By Erin Yoshikawa and Mirren Hogan

Even in the distant future, there are pests everywhere you go. From Earth's moon to Pluto and Alpha Centauri, there was always a nuisance creature ready to be a pain in someone's ass. They ranged from tiny microbes that itched and stung to giant cockroaches that could jump fifty metres in the air. Most were relatively harmless, save for their numbers.

But every few thousand species, one came along that could pose a serious threat to humans abroad in outer space.

On board the SS O'Kearney, a luxury space liner, the wine cellar was far from quiet. It was odd, considering the general lack of noise in space. It started out as a tipped bottle from one of the pneumatic wine racks. Not a big deal – the webbing that held them in place during hyperspace travel was worn and needed replacing. The repair and maintenance team took care of the job between Jupiter and Venus.

A cask of Amontillado turned up empty the day before a large event. That was surprising since the ship's records had reported it full at deployment. But there were other casks, and the passengers didn't think anything of it. However, the supply manager was beginning to wonder about the sudden loss of gallons of wine.

Therefore, they sent one of the inventory specialists down into the wine cellar. It was dark and cool, the environment carefully controlled to keep the precious cargo at its peak. The only light came from a series of units that dotted the walls and gave off a soft, yellow glow reminiscent of candles made from wax procured out of Earth's endangered bee population. As one came close, the light flickered on and snuffed itself out when the body passed. At the far end of the corridor, between hundreds of bottles and casks, the lights switched on and off, as if someone was moving past them.

Tanya Markins jumped slightly. She wasn't normally unnerved being down here, but today was different. Today it had a peculiar feeling of being occupied. That made no sense. Still, she called out, "Hello?"

A soft baritone voice lilted from behind a row of gigantic barrels of whiskey. "Hello, there. What's a pretty thing like you doing in a place like this?" She jumped. "Who's there?"

"Just a man looking for the good stuff. But with such a fine selection, I could never choose just one tipple." The hair on his head was bright red and messy, but his clothes were fine. Perhaps a little out of date, cut to the old standards of Earth's bright yesteryear, but the green waistcoat and dark jacket were made of fine material. Even his shoes were polished to a mirror shine, and his smile was equally as bright. "Do you suggest anything, miss... ?"

"I suggest you should be on the passenger quarters, not down in storage." Or the brig, if he'd stowed away in here. She brushed back a strand of dark hair from her eyes. "Look, if you need directions—"

"Directions, yes!" The man clapped large hands together and stepped forward. He was very tall, with pale skin gone ruddy at the tip of his nose and largish ears. With a rather handsome face and charming smile, he looked like a European dandy attempting to go retro in his fashion choices. "Where do you keep the Beaujolais? I'm in the mood for something delicate and sweet."

"How about I show you the door instead?" she suggested. "It's possible you've had enough to drink already." Why did some passengers have to be difficult?

"Lovely girl," the man drawled, "there's no such thing as enough to drink. Not for me, anyway." He started to come closer, the lights flickering on and off as he walked in a surprisingly straight line towards the woman. "I know where the door is. But I much prefer the view from here.”

“I’m sure. Look I—you really can’t be in here.” She was starting to feel strangely giddy. “Why don’t you come with me?”

“But I still haven’t found my drink,” the man protested, “or your name. I’m not leaving without those two things.”

“Try coffee from the mess,” Tanya replied, her voice tight.

He caught her gently by the hand and tugged her towards him. He smelled faintly of oak barrels and rich leather. “Give me your name first.”

His touch was like a jolt of electricity. It sent her heart racing. “Tanya,” she said.

“Hello, Tanya.” He raised her hand and kissed the soft skin of her wrist. “Call me Clurichaun.”

“That’s an… interesting name,” she replied.

Clurichaun chuckled and pulled her closer to his body. “A few women have also called me their god. Would you like to know why?”

She snorted in a soft expression of disbelief. “Why?”

His smile was devious as his hands began to wander down to her hips. “Let me show you.”

“Why would I want to do that?” she asked. She wanted to, but she really didn’t know why herself. Maybe it was because of the long period of celibacy due to the lack of decent men on this tiny ship.

“Because, why not?”

She didn’t answer that.

Clurichaun chuckled quietly as he pressed thin lips over the woman’s. The oak barrel and leather smell was musky and dark, like a fine cologne. It pervaded the air as he claimed Tanya's mouth, his tongue darting out to press for entry.

She opened her mouth and tasted wine, coupled with something else unidentifiable. Perhaps the flavour of the forbidden.

While their lips were locked together, his hands began to undo the layers of clothing that held Tanya's body from view. He worked swiftly, shedding the garments without breaking contact. When she was naked, he finally pulled away and drank in the delicious sight. "I never get tired of a woman's body," he whispered, before dropping to his knees in front of her.

"What if someone comes?" she asked, looking toward the doorway.

"They might learn a trick or two." He quickly buried his face between her thighs and ran his tongue across the hair on Tanya's mound.

She moaned with the sudden jolt of pleasure.

"Delicious," Clurichaun breathed, before dipping his tongue into the apex of her sex. His hands urged her thighs apart, letting her know there were sweeter treasures in store if she dared to take them.

Of course she dared. She went one better by bending a knee, opening herself to him.

He made a sound like a big cat's purr and hooked a large hand under her bent knee. He took a deep breath and blew it out gently, his eyes transfixed on the thatch of unruly curls. With her sex exposed, Clurichaun began to dance his tongue over the soft outer lips to tease more of Tanya's sweet juices from her.

She moaned again. "I think I understand now."

Clurichaun chuckled and buried his face deeper between the woman's thighs. He only touched her clit every third of four strokes, a tease meant to drive Tanya to absolute distraction.

"Please... " she panted.

He stood and wrapped her thigh around his hip. Something hard and hot was pressed against the woman's belly, throbbing softly against her skin. "Please what?"

"I think you know what." She started trying to undo his pants with trembling fingers.

"Maybe," he whispered against her ear, "but I'm very vain. Say it for me? Please?" He pressed himself harder against Tanya, but took both of her hands away from his trousers.

"I want you," she said without reservation.

"Good lass." With one swift thrust, he was deep inside her. Tanya didn't have a chance to think about when Clurichaun had undone his pants, but he was there, hitting just the right spots and grinding into her with easy movements of his hips.

She moaned, louder this time. "Oh yes!"

Her pleasure spurred him on. He moved harder and faster inside her, his breath hissing past Tanya's ear as lungs worked overtime to keep up. Deft fingers wound down her body, wiping away the sheen of sweat that had begun to form. One hand slithered between their bodies and pressed against the spot where they joined. "I need to hear you let go, lass." Clurichaun grated out words from between clenched teeth. "Do it for me?"

"No, not yet," she panted.

His chuckle was dark and rich like honeyed mead. "Don't worry, lass. There's more to come. But I need to hear you."

"Mmm." She couldn't resist any longer. She moaned, long and high as she climaxed hard and sweet.

He went as deep as possible, letting Tanya ride the waves of pleasure until they slowed. As soon as he felt her body relax, he dropped down to his knees and buried his mouth between her thighs again.

She lowered her leg to the floor and took a breath. Even with such a strong orgasm, she was still aroused. In fact, she was more aroused now than she'd been before.

There was no slow tease, this time. He attacked her swollen lips and clit with his tongue, her juices covering his chin. Clurichaun groaned against her hot flesh, his own ardour pressed firmly against Tanya's smooth calf as he delved deep into her hot core.

It only took her moments to climax again, gasping and shuddering with pleasure. It left her feeling even more aroused.

He drew away with a wide grin on his wet lips, green eyes darting towards a cask of fruit brandy. Clurichaun stood briskly and grabbed Tanya's hand to lead her to it. He spun the woman and pressed her down so she was laid out across the large barrel, her pert rear on display.

"Hold on," he whispered. With one smooth stroke, Clurichaun drove deep inside her again, his hands steely around her hips as he moved with determination.

She gasped with this new sensation, smooth wood beneath her, him deeply inside her. "Oh my gosh. Harder, please," she begged. "Deeper."

He was nothing if not an obliging servant to a lady's wishes. Sweat rolled down from his temples as Clurichaun drove on, giving the woman little chance to catch her breath. A hot hand slid from Tanya's waist down between her smooth thighs. His fingers pressed against her clit and massaged it, forcing more moans of pleasure from the woman.

She came again, harder than ever, but still her desire was far from sated.

Most men would have called it quits by now, but not Clurichaun. He was made of something entirely different from mere mortals. If the lady wanted him to go straight into the next twenty-four hour cycle, that's what he was going to do.

He pulled away from Tanya and proceeded to turn her around. With one hand, he spread her thighs apart while the other positioned his cock for another round. Never let it be said that Clurichaun left a lady...

"Oy! Tanya! You all right in here?" A deep voice boomed from the entrance, followed by the flicker of lights as someone stepped down into the hold.

"Fuck," she whispered. Out loud, she called, "I'm fine, thanks."

"What're you doing? Did you figure out where all the booze went?" Lights flickered on and off as the speaker came towards their hiding spot.

Clurichaun made a shushing gesture to keep Tanya quiet. "Not a word about me, lass. Time for me to be gone." He kissed her one more time with an expression of regret before backing away into the shadows. This time, instead of the lights coming on, the walkway remained dark.

"Nuno," she said more loudly than intended.

"Tanya? Where are—Aaaahhh!" There was a scream followed by a sound suspiciously like Clurichaun's chuckle. "Who in hell are you?" Asked the first man.

"Just a pest. But it looks like it's time for me to jump ship. Y'might wanna consider stopping off at Europa for a resupply. Wine's going bad." There was a brief rustle before all the lights went out in the hold.

"Wait!" Tanya scrambled off the barrel and felt around for her clothes. "Don't go."

"Wait, I'll get the lights but it's gonna take me a minute." The man scrambled about in the dark for the backup switches. It took more than a minute, but that also meant Tanya had enough time to get dressed.

"There," He shouted triumphantly from three aisles away, "we must have burnt a fuse out. Where are you, Tanya?"

"Here." She was sitting next to a barrel, dressed but staring blankly in front of her.

"Bit of a shock, finding someone down here. Don't think he was on the passenger list, either. Where'd that bastard go?" The man, Anthony, SS O'Kearney's quartermaster, stared down at her with real concern. "Not looking so good, girl. Need a drink? Or were you doing that already?"

"I wasn't drinking. I must have fallen asleep."

"I'm not gonna ask... " Anthony shook his head and went to pick out two bottles from a rack across from Tanya. His nose wrinkled as a sour smell hit his sensitive nose. "Are we keeping vinegar down here?"

"Probably," she replied. "Wine doesn't last forever." Once it went bad it smelt horrible.

"Of course, but... " Anthony did the unthinkable: he put a bottle's cork between his teeth and yanked it from the bung. "Smell this." Anthony held it to Tanya's nose, but the stench was strong enough to be smelt from across the room.

She grimaced. "That smells very off," she said. "I think it needs to be thrown away. How odd."